THE BRIDE PRICE
BY GRETE WEIL

translated by John Barrett

Grete Weil invests the Old Testament's dry bones with flesh and blood, in a vivid seance that resonates across the centuries to our own time.

In this strikingly original novel, Grete Weil intertwines two narratives — one a moving recreation of a Biblical story, and the other a haunting testimony of her own experiences as a survivor of the Holocaust.

The first, the story of King David, is told by his first wife Michal. A shadowy figure whom David curses in the Bible, Michal, in Weil's recounting, is a compassionate figure, a woman appalled at the violence that has occasioned her marriage, but who nevertheless remains emotionally bound to her brilliant and powerful husband. As prophecies and politics disfigure David, Michal begins to question the mercy and wisdom of the Lord and His anointed. Her world is evoked with a broad imagination: we see her as a girl, firmly devoted to her older brother Jonathan; as the horrified pawn of her mad and maddening father; as the target of her rival, Bathsheba; as, finally, aging and ruminative, a woman whose voice, never hysterical, never shrill, persists above the clashes and struggles of husbands, brothers, and fathers.

In brilliant counterpoint, Weil tells her own story, that of a survivor of the Holocaust

(continued on back flap)

The Bride Price

The Bride Price

A NOVEL BY
Grete Weil

TRANSLATED FROM THE GERMAN
BY JOHN BARRETT

DAVID R. GODINE, PUBLISHER, INC.
BOSTON

First published in English in 1991 by
DAVID R. GODINE, PUBLISHER, INC.
Horticultural Hall
300 Massachusetts Avenue
Boston, Massachusetts 02115

Originally published in German in 1988 by
Verlag Nagel and Kimche AG

Library of Congress Cataloging-in-Publication Data
Weil, Grete, 1906–
[Brautpreis. English]
The bride price : a novel / by Grete Weil ;
translated from the German by John Barrett. — 1st ed.
p.   cm.
Translation of: Der Brautpreis.
ISBN 0-87923-893-3
I. Title.
PT2647.E4157B713   1991
833'.914—dc20   91-7146   CIP

FIRST EDITION
Printed in the United States of America

for
BERND ALTMEYER,
without whose help as a fellow human and physician
this book would not have been written.

Translator's Note

The New Oxford Annotated Bible has been used as the basis for the scriptural excerpts and the Dictionary of Scripture Proper Names in *Webster's New Twentieth Century Dictionary* as the standard for the English spelling of the biblical names used in the original German version of the book.

The biblical quotations used by Grete Weil were taken from the German translation of the Bible by Martin Buber and Franz Rosenzweig. Where the Oxford Bible quotations differ slightly from the German version, adjustment toward the German wording has been made.

The Bride Price

❧ *I,* GRETE, with the two German, two Christian names Margarete Elisabeth, was shown Michelangelo's David by my father, in an art book. He stroked the page lovingly and said: "Il Gigante." I liked the word; I was a word-fetishist, if one moved me with its sound, I became addicted to it. Naturally I already knew from the monologue of the Maid of Orleans: "who once chose Jesse's devout son, the shepherd, to be his warrior," that David had been a shepherd boy who conquered the giant Goliath with his sling. So he could not have been a giant himself or his deed would not have been so astonishing. Then I read that the huge marble block from which the young sculptor had carved his figure of the youth had already been named "il Gigante" by its previous owner, Agostino di Duccio, and he had intended to sculpt a David from it, but the plan had to be given up because the colossus had been damaged in transport from Carrara to Florence. The name stayed with the stone, Michelangelo took up the challenge and made from it the young David, the beautiful, the unconquerable, the hero whom I admired at a time when I did not know what misfortune heroes mean for the world.

My fifteen-year-old schoolmates bought photos of the youthful favorite of our State Theater, fastened them to the wall with thumbtacks, carried them around in their pockets, or tore them into little pieces and ate them in wild passion. Chance kept me from such excesses: I had met that actor, so impetuously adored by my girlfriends, at friends of my parents, a polite, faintly melancholy young man with a face that was lightly made-up and a pleasant baritone voice, certainly attractive, nothing more. No photos of Andreas Traxel in my room. Instead, three of the Gigante, 24 by 30, black and white, in silky matte-finish, the entire figure, the head with its curled lips *en face* and in three-quarter profile. To look at, to love. Beauty absolute. A yokel. A son of peasants. Resolved, courageous. Weighing his possibilities, but capable of anything.

I don't know whether I had already heard anything about homoerotic love by that time, but I painted the beginning of Platen's "Tristan": "Whoever has looked upon beauty with his eyes is already given over to death," in calligraphy on a piece of parchment and fastened it to the wall beside the Gigante, because I sensed that both belonged together.

Dialogue at twilight: you are not yet a victor, but you soon will be. You are only waiting for the right moment to destroy Goliath, that which is dark, evil. You have the power, know your strength; from a branch you have carved the sling for yourself and gathered stones from the bed of the stream. The deed is not yet done. But the dream that precedes it has been dreamed. By you and by me.

Things stayed that way for a long time. My hero did not

change, I changed. Grew up. I did not connect David with anything Jewish. He was a Florentine and *basta*.

I wanted to be German, not Jewish. Sat in the Jewish religion class and dreamed of Egmont, the Prince of Homburg, Don Carlos. We learned to rattle off Hebrew prayers from memory without knowing any Hebrew.

About Judaism I learned what amounted to nothing at all, at home as well as at school. A person who lives through her eyes can't do anything with a religion that rejects the image.

I was still secure in my parents' house. I still just turned my head away when they sang: "When Jewish blood spurts from the knife." I still said without hesitating: Bavaria, my homeland.

Did we know that things would not go well? Deep in our unconscious, the past: scorn, persecution, banishment, murder. But no stink of Auschwitz in the nose. The unthinkable not yet thought.

Jews are used to being pessimistic. From experience, instinct. We were pessimistic. But imagination does not suffice for knowing about your own annihilation in advance. Not then. Today we are smarter. Anything is possible.

Then: growing uneasiness, but still no fear. We were Germans. Germans and Jews. It is enriching to stem from two roots. Cool north and hot Mediterranean. What came of it was often talent—for mathematics, physics, music, for writing. As well as for medicine and financial transactions. Accompanied by a certain arrogance that comes from belonging to the chosen people. Chosen for what? For suffering above all.

Belief, search for God, piety. That was foreign to me.

Then I began to think about the fact that David had been a Jew. That made me proud. I did not inquire further into his history. Knew nothing more than that he had slain Goliath and was king between Saul and Solomon.

At one point in those years I took a trip to Holland with my brother. I was crazy about the mountains and did not like the lowlands. I wouldn't have believed anyone who prophesied that here I would eventually spend twelve years, the most decisive and most bitter of my life, and would come to love the flat country under its huge, vivid sky together with its people who looked so gray to me in their raincoats. Then, in the Hague, in the Mauritshuis, I stood in front of a David, Rembrandt's David, who was so very different from mine but moved me regardless, more than any picture had ever moved me before. A little Jewish boy is playing the harp before the tall, powerful, turban-crowned King Saul, who has been so deeply moved that he is half concealing himself behind a curtain and wiping a tear from his eye. David, no hero, a poet and singer, why hadn't I ever thought of that? I became a traitress to my beautiful one. This dark-haired, rather ugly boy displaced the warrior, he, the brother of many from Amsterdam's Jewish quarter, who still lived there and were named Judah, Benjamin, Ruben, Abraham, or even David, who were not kings but merchants, diamond cutters, Talmud students, occasionally musicians—and of whom scarcely one survived.

I bought a large color print of the Rembrandt picture and put it up at home beside Michelangelo's David. There they were together, the two extremes of humanity, and I sat in front of them, my head propped on my hands, more uncertain than in Holland, carried away again by the beauty, but with the premonition that the little one, the ugly one, the artist, fit better into my world.

Michelangelo and Rembrandt, both had given form to a part of David as he has come down to us from the Bible, belonging half to history, half to myth, ruling for forty years, at first just over Judah, then over all Israel at the beginning of the millennium before the birth of Christ, a great hero, a great poet, later a great king.

I began to doubt, to mistrust the historians, the chroniclers. David could be anything: saint and criminal, singer and murderer, lover of men, despiser of men, wise man and fool. What was he?

I, MICHAL, daughter of King Saul, twice wife of King David and one of his widows, live in the palace of his son Solomon, close to my enemy Bathsheba. Her old hatred, her desire for revenge. Revenge for what? It was she who took David away from me. Someday she will have me done away with, and even if there is not much to be said for my old woman's life between house and garden, garden and house, I am still frightened of losing it. Afraid of every bite that I eat, every mouthful that I drink, and of every strange footstep and owe it to this fear that I am still alive: Bathsheba knows it and enjoys it to the fullest. When I am dead, she will have done away with her pleasure in tormenting me.

In order to restrain my fear, I sit in the shade of the olive tree, watch the play of colors in the glittering green and silver leaves moving in the wind, and tell my story to myself.

I tell it to myself even at night in my bed, when I cannot sleep and can think of nothing else but in what manner she will do it, whether she will have me stabbed, choked, or poisoned. Flickering light, shadows that move. The living or ghosts?

Alone with fear. It is always there. Follows me at every step. Like the puppy Jeffi that my brother Jonathan brought for me when I was really still just a child. What a comparison. As if I loved my fear. I loved Jeffi, she was taken away from me because animals were not to be kept in the house. My first pain. I cried for days.

And yet: full of longing I think of the time when we left our tents to live in permanent houses, when everything was breaking up, a nomadic people becoming settled. To our advantage, to our disadvantage. We, the royal family, the generals and courtiers, took on fine manners, used cutlery for eating instead of our fingers, wore more beautiful clothing and richer jewelry. Learned to speak Egyptian. But distanced ourselves from the people and thereby lost our knowledge of animals and plants.

We no longer went on foot, rode asses; several sons of the rich had brought mules along with them from abroad, Jahwe does not permit us to pair unlike creatures. Only Jonathan, heir to the throne, possesses a horse, the black stallion Eran. Eran, the Vigilant—we thought up the name together. I beg my parents to get me a horse as well, am put off: impossible for a girl. So we both ride on Eran, I sit behind Jonathan and hold fast to him. His dark hair blows in my face, excites me and calms me. When we get off to let the overheated animal drink at a spring or a brook, I lay my head against my brother's breast and we kiss each other. Passionately, tenderly, like husband and wife. I would have been fourteen or fifteen years old then, no one knows exactly, and when I ask my mother, Ahinoam, she laughs and brusquely spits out: "Doesn't matter with a daughter. I forget."

He was beautiful, my Jonathan, slender and tall, even if not so incredibly tall as our father, with broad shoulders, narrow hips, a friendly face and strong hands that I could always depend on. Saul's firstborn and I, the youngest, very far apart, three brothers and Merab, our sister, between us.

Far below the city, in the low-lying region through which, in winter, flows a brook that dries up in summer, we sit in front of Jonathan's tent where he is still more at home than in his house. Our favorite spot. He says a bit sadly: "In Egypt the Pharaohs marry their sisters. We can't do that. Jahwe has forbidden it." The first time that I bruise myself on one of Jahwe's commandments. I am devout, like all people I know, permeated by the certainty that the world belongs to Jahwe, our Lord, and that he has chosen us, us alone, to serve Him.

I take Jonathan's hand. "It must please Jahwe, if two who love each other remain together." "Not when they are brother and sister." "How do you know that?" He hesitates a moment, then he says with confidence: "The prophets proclaim it, they know the will of Jahwe." "And if they are deceived?" I am frightened. Sense that I have touched a forbidden thing.

Jonathan takes his hand away. I cry.

Then fear. I have insulted the prophets. Jahwe would perhaps forgive me, not Samuel. Our prophet, Moses' legitimate successor. Must he learn of my blasphemy? Mistrust of him who is closest to me, of Jonathan. My gentle brother can be made to tell. Samuel hears the evidence. Judges. Condemns. Samuel rules. We obey. The old, emaciated man in clothing of undyed linen, with the pinched mouth and small, mean eyes. Once upon a time, he anointed our father, a peasant's son who had gone out to look for runaway asses, as king, not voluntarily, for the first time in his life coerced by the people, who were more and more passionately demanding a leader against the Philistines. He chose Saul because he was the tallest, towered over all the others, was good-humored in addition, a willing tool. A few drops of oil on his forehead and right after that a speech against the royalty that he himself had actually just introduced. He called it a betrayal of Jahwe, the only legitimate king.

Just recently a terrible thing had happened. Saul had conquered and exterminated the Amalekites, but, against Samuel's, or as he naturally claimed, against Jahwe's express command, had spared the life of their King Agag. Nor had Father, who had once been a farmer, wanted to kill the large herds of sheep and cattle. So the old prophet slew the defenseless Agag with his own hand. It is said that Samuel cursed Saul in the name of Jahwe, and said that the Lord had rejected him as king and had already chosen another who would soon wear the crown. Father returns from Gilgal to Gibeah, distraught, trembles with rage if someone contradicts him, beats the slaves, wanders restlessly through the palace with tortured, roving eyes, of which I am afraid.

One time Jonathan and I return home, meet our weeping mother in the palace. "Your father," she says, "has lost his mind. Again and again he hurls his spear at the wall and screams that he will destroy the brazen usurper who has sneaked off with Jahwe's love. He is fighting with the air, there is no one who threatens him. I have summoned the physicians, they are as helpless as I am."

We ascend the stairs, two guards are standing in front of the throne room: "On order of the physicians, Prince Jonathan may not enter. In his madness the king could take him to be the one who wants to steal the throne from him. Princess Michal may enter."

Semidarkness inside, father, no longer raving, is lying on his bed and sobbing. I stroke his head. He does not notice me. One of the physicians takes me by the shoulder: "He will soon sleep. We have given him a potion that calms and makes one sleepy." The sobbing becomes softer, father's powerful body twitches a few more times. Then quiet. With lowered voices, the physicians advise what is to be done. Animals should be sacrificed, the king should be infused with wine, cedar wood should be placed on his chest, he should be washed with the water of the brook, smeared with the red dye of the shield-louse; one considers it beneficial to put a young woman into his bed. Eleazar, the gray-haired one, whom alone I would have for my physician if I were sick, strokes his beard as he says: "Music. Music will help him." I listen closely. The physicians shake their heads, the eldest asks scornfully: "Perhaps the trumpets that caused the walls of Jericho to collapse?" Eleazar smiles. Says that his daughter has married in Bethlehem. There is a young shepherd there who often grazes his father's sheep beside her house and sings at the same time. When he, Eleazar, visits his daughter, he listens to the youth and thereby forgets everything he had intended to do that day, often even the telling of stories to his grandchildren as he had promised. "How is he called?" asks one of them. "David."

For the first time I hear the name of the one who will be my destiny, whom I shall love, for whom I shall long, whom I shall curse. Who kept me from becoming what I was, a rebel who revolts against religion, against the compulsion to explain every misdeed that one perpetrates with the words: Jahwe has willed it. No one has said it more often than David. Empty words: Jahwe has willed it. To wage wars, kill people, plunge them into misery. Jahwe has willed it. This frightful God. But why did I let myself be hindered, why did I give way if David so much as looked at me? Seduced by the gleam of his gray, slanting eyes, carried away by passion, I belonged not to myself, but to him, a woman, his woman, who denied herself to him, who desired him. This fearful love. He knew it, took advantage of it, said laughingly or softly or even harshly: Jahwe does not want women to mix in the affairs of men.

Finally the physicians agree with Eleazar. They could at least try this David and his songs.

When I tell Jonathan, he smiles sadly: "A singing youth. How will that help the king?"

With that he leaves. He does not live in the palace, has his own house, wife, and children. That has no bearing on our love. His marriage is duty. The successor to the throne must have heirs.

A few days later I see him again. Changed, beaming. He laughs, takes me in his arms in front of all the people and kisses me on the mouth. "Are you drunk?" "No. Yes. But not from wine." "In love, then?" It is bitter, to ask that. Jonathan nods: "Up till now I have had no idea how wonderful that is." Nearly in tears I ask: "Who?" He puts his mouth close to my ear and whispers: "David."

Thus the name strikes me for the second time, hard and heavy. Love for a sister may be halfway permissible, love for another man is a sin. I feel hatred. Yes, hatred is the first thing that I feel at the mention of the name David. I would like to kill him, strangle him, scratch out the eyes that have bewitched Jonathan. But already another feeling is added: curiosity, which blends into the wish also to love the one whom Jonathan loves.

My brother puts his arm around my shoulder: "You must see and hear him, Michal, Jahwe's angel, more beautiful, more exalted than man has ever been. Father has had another attack. David is playing his harp now. Come with me."

We dare not enter the throne room, remain standing outside, pressed close to one another, and listen. The sound of the harp, exulting, different from anything ever heard before, above it a strong man's voice that hums, that sings, that glorifies without words. It demands, it bestows, climbs to heaven, returns to earth, full of lust for battle, yet full of piety as well. I begin to fly, to glide away through time and space, beyond myself, back to myself. My eternity.

The fall from the clouds. There is talking inside. Jonathan leads me away. Saul may not know that we have been here.

He had become Jahwe's angel for me as well, even before I had seen him. I did not want to see him at all. I wanted to hear him. Possess him with my ears. Music, music. There was no longer anything else. The most splendid, the most liberating thing. And he the embodiment.

I loiter near the throne room. Father confers with his advisers, with Abner, the Commander-in-Chief. A king has much to do. Things that do not interest me, things that are earthbound. But I long to be lifted into the sky again.

If I could turn back time, that is where I would stop it. When I loved him without having to suffer because of him. When he was only a voice for me.

I do not know where David lives. Somewhere with the servants. He is healing the king, yet he is treated like the slave who binds up Saul's sandals.

And again: father bellows like a flayed animal. Father weeps. I tremble with joy. Now David has to sing. And I can hear him.

This time I am alone, without Jonathan, do not remain standing outside, lift the curtain, slip into the hall. Crouch in a corner with my eyes closed. Today he sings words: "Lift up your heads, O gates! and be lifted up, O ancient doors! that the King of Glory may come in."

My eyes are moist, but the words hold me tightly, I cannot fly. Slowly I open my eyes and see him. There he stands, the harp on his arm, slender and supple, more a youth than a man, in a white shirt with blue fringes along the lower border, the blond hair falling to his shoulders. I stand up, now he sees me, looks at me with his gray eyes. A smile twitches at the corners of his ample mouth, a bold, desiring smile.

And he sings on: "Who is this King of Glory? The Lord of Hosts, he is the King of Glory! on high!"

Rejoicing everywhere. Father sits upon the throne, his two hands grasp the armrests. His face is relaxed, looks as it did in earlier days, near and familiar, he resembles Jonathan at this moment. He looks at David full of love and smiles.

He does not notice me. I leave the hall quietly.

Now I am aware of my love. And begin to suffer. Dream that I am lying in his arms. Childish fantasies, far removed from reality. Just the first premonition of physical happiness. And my love for Jonathan? I do not understand myself any longer. At an age when love is the absolute, I pronounce judgment upon myself: faithless. One cannot love two men. Not at the same time.

O Jahwe, help. But he does not help and I begin to doubt that this invisible power, which has created heaven and earth, discovered by us and called God, is even willing or able to give me, Michal, a sign. There is no sign. Nothing.

Two days later Jonathan. I embrace him and weep a little. "I love him. Love him so very much." He strokes my hair. "That is good. The two people who are dearest to me love one another. Since he saw you, he talks of nothing but you. I will take you to him, make yourself beautiful. But cut the bells from your sandals. We must not be heard. We will ride." "Where?" He puts his hand on my mouth. As the good, familiar smell of his skin enters my nose, I know that I love him and will always love him, just like David, know that one can love two men at the same time. I change my clothing, drop oil of myrrh between my breasts, that suddenly appear too small to me, hang a three-stranded chain of seashells around my neck and put a pomegranate blossom in my hair.

We leave the city, ride downward, reach Jonathan's tent. Flapping lightly like sails, the canvas surfaces beat against each other. Jonathan dismounts, lifts me from the horse and stakes Eran fast. Within a torch is burning. On the couch of brightly colored carpets David is lying, in his white shirt with the blue fringes. He leaps up, embraces Jonathan. They kiss a long time, I stand to the side, helpless, angry. Has my brother brought me along to demonstrate his strange love to me? I am superfluous, unnoticed, a spectator who has no business being here, I want to get away, far away. Then they let each other go, David comes over to me, I see only his eyes, their great brightness, their irises contracting in the unsteady light. He takes my hands and presses them to his mouth. When he releases me, Jonathan has gone. We are alone. Sit on the couch, hand in hand, and say: you are beautiful, you are dear, you are good, say David and Michal, Michal and David, call each other evening star, rose blossom, summer wind, mate of the butterfly. He produces a flute, says: This I cut for myself in Bethlehem, watching my sheep. And begins to play. Longing, tenderness, wooing, desire. The music envelops me, carries me off, I am flying again. We fall upon the couch, I feel myself, I feel him, life and death so close together, frenzy, and finally exhaustion and sleep.

I had an entire lifetime to think it over, whether David loved me in the beginning. Whether the king's daughter was not just a rung on the ladder that he was climbing. Probably that too. But he loved me that night, of that I am certain. I could have been a shepherd girl or a slave. The song that he played for me on his flute was a love song. The song was he himself.

His love slipped away like his music in the uncertain life of the fugitive that faced him. Yet he had me summoned after he was king. He could not tolerate any loss, I had been taken away from him, he wanted to have me back again. It did him good that I shared his life, in spite of Abigail and the other wives, I remained the first. Until Bathsheba came. He died in her arms, not in mine. I do not want to think about that. I want to remember the David of the first night, the lover, the only one to whom I could give myself. If fate means well with me, the song of the flute will resound in me again at the hour of my death.

My brother had promised to take me to David again one evening, but it never came to that. On that day the Philistines fell upon our land again, an entirely new period began: David's rise, David's fame, he became a hero and a hero is what I got for a husband in the end, though I had wished for a singer.

Jonathan took his farewell from us; from David I heard

nothing. But I had no doubt that he would go into battle. He had to show the world what sort of a man he was.

We were used to wars. There was always a war. The Amalek-ites, the Ammonites, and, most often, the Philistines attacked us. Or we them, it was hard to tell exactly which.

Now, under Solomon, there is peace. David defeated all our enemies so thoroughly that Solomon can reign in peace, erect his stately buildings, and spread his fame as the wisest of kings. Formerly—when I was a child and my father ruled— the outcome of battle was often uncertain and the women lived in constant fear: What would happen if our enemies defeated us? Would they ravish us? Carry us off to slavery? Do away with us?

Even before we had settled in Canaan, the Philistines had been there. A people that had come from over the sea, that lived on the coast. Not without culture, but foreign, different from us, with different features, with other customs, other gods. We called them the foreskinned ones, scornfully, dispar-agingly, as if it were a disgrace that their men still had what was taken away from our little boys with a flint knife.

At the same time, our soldiers, at least, were dependent on the Philistines. They provided us with the weapons with which we fought them. In peacetime, the dulled swords were taken back to them so that they could be sharpened. We gave them grain, sometimes gold as well and in return they gave us iron armor and iron swords. Before that time we had only had weapons of copper. The iron of the Philistines was better. Better for protection, better for killing.

And now our swordsmiths had fallen upon us once again. Why? Perhaps in addition to the grain we gave them, they also wanted to have the ground on which it grew, the desert that we had made fruitful. Perhaps they were afraid of our different ways, our belief in Jahwe. Reasons for war were quickly found, they were readily at hand, you had only to give them a name. Fear was always part of it, but it was never called that. Who likes to admit that he is afraid?

Messengers reported that the two armies were standing opposite each other on the sides of the wide lowland area in front of Bethlehem, the city of David's birth. Neither dared to attack. Then the enemy proposed a duel instead of battle and bade his chosen warrior, a giant by the name of Goliath, come forward. If he were defeated by a Hebrew—highly improbable that these puny men would defeat a giant—then the Philistines would withdraw. If he won, well, everyone knew what would happen.

Saul sought desperately for a volunteer for the battle. The king promised gifts to the one who would risk it: freedom from all tributes and, when no one volunteered, the hand of a daughter.

So simple. The hand of a daughter. To some ruffian. Who possibly was ugly, had no manners, stank. A curse, to be a daughter. Mother and Merab began to cry. The only weapon at their disposal. I was quite calm. Just thought if I am that daughter I will run away. Together with David. In that instant I realized that David could be the one. In order to have me for his wife. My darling with the delicate harp-player's hands. That could not be. I racked my brain, nothing of use occurred to me. Just stupid ideas. Send a messenger to father: take back your promise. Neither Merab nor I are prepared to be given to some warrior or other. It would not make the least impression upon him. Women have to obey. Such is the will of Jahwe, who created Eve from Adam's rib.

Only one thing left for me: ride. To ride to the army at Bethlehem and keep David from the battle. Flee with him. Somewhere where there are no giants and no wars. Jonathan must help me. He loves him too. A new fear: my brother will not permit David's battle with the monster and will sacrifice himself.

I go out quietly, down to the stables, where Eran is standing in the midst of many asses. I command a servant to put on the bridle. "This instant?" "Yes, this instant." "Prince Jonathan is not here." "I will ride alone." He shrugs his shoulders and does what I tell him. I mount and ride in the direction of the sun, where Bethlehem must lie.

Then I see people coming out of all the streets, forcing their way up to the palace. They are shouting, rejoicing. Suddenly I pick out the word David. Believe that I can distinguish it. But who knows him? Because I am thinking of nothing else but David, the word echoes toward me a hundred times.

Eran shies from the crowd, rears up on his hind legs, gallops back to the stable. The youth lifts me down. "What are they yelling about?" I ask. "They are shouting: David. David. David has slain Goliath."

They shout it again and again, the whole day. They shout it my whole life long. They will continue to shout it after hundreds, after thousands of years: David has slain Goliath. The dwarf the giant. Spirit brute force.

Did David slay Goliath? Yes, well, yes, perhaps. I do not know for sure. Probably no one knows. Was Goliath already dead when the stone from the sling penetrated his skull?

David always boasted of never having killed a man with his own hands, as if it mattered whether you did the killing yourself or gave the order to have it done. When I scoffingly asked him in later years what happened to Goliath, he nervously tented his right eyebrow and said with contempt: "That was not a man. That was an animal."

Well, yes. For a while, I saw it that way myself. When I still believed that through Goliath's death I had come closer to my goal of becoming David's wife.

David stays with the men who are pursuing the fleeing Philistines, but Jonathan comes back. He has greeted his wife, his children, has been to our mother, has me summoned and takes Eran out of his stall. And again we are in his tent, he stretches out on his bed and says: "I am tired, Michal. War is a foreign condition for me. I like to look on, observe, deliberate. Then I feel that I am alive. In war I am dead." My tall brother, who does not want to be a hero. Who is Israel's good, Israel's true soul.

He smiles: "But I still want to tell you the story, as it really was. Before it becomes a legend."

Jonathan and David with the army. Inseparable. Even at night they sleep under the same piece of tenting. While Saul is looking for a warrior to oppose Goliath, David has disappeared for the whole day. Comes back in the evening in a cheerful mood. Says he has been visiting old Eleazar, his patron. A wise man, this Eleazar, a physician who knows about giants and dwarfs. Unbridled laughter. Then a command. You, Jonathan, when the sun rises tomorrow, will take up your position facing Goliath. Face him, not fight him. No closer to him than ten paces shall you go. What is the purpose of that, asks Jonathan. But David remains silent.

At daybreak they leave camp. Jonathan in armor, his sword in his hand. David trots along beside him, barefoot, in his white shirt, with a sling. As they come to the brook that divides the plain, he picks up a few large, smooth stones. What are you doing? Oh, nothing, just for amusement. Jonathan walks on, crosses the brook, comes to the Philistines' side. Then David is no longer beside him. A sudden emptiness. Jonathan walks farther, the rising sun at his back. Loudly he calls for Goliath. He comes out of his tent, terrifyingly huge, a giant, uncouth, in iron armor. What do you want, he asks. Do battle with you. The monster laughs. The voice with which he says: come here, you dwarf, is astonishingly high and pinched. Slowly, with his sword held out in front, Jonathan walks toward him. Stops ten paces distant from him. Have you lost your courage, Jew? taunts the huge one. Then, from the left, quite close by, comes the cry of a bird. Goliath turns his head. Jonathan seizes this tiny moment, leaps forward, and thrusts the sword into his neck beneath the ear which had been uncovered by his turning. Simultaneously, or nearly simultaneously, a stone flies, smashes through Goliath's helmet and forehead. And now David is at Jonathan's side, the laughing David. You? says Jonathan. Then he reacts quickly, picks up the dead man's sword and gives it to David. Cut off his head. Take it to Saul. You, David, have killed Goliath, you alone. David is no longer laughing. Naturally I alone. Who else? It was foolish of you to come so close. I was not in danger. Old Eleazar revealed to me that many giants have a growth in their heads that narrows their field of vision. So I came from the side and tricked him with the bird call.

Jonathan sits up, takes my hand: "Michal, when David had cut off Goliath's head and was standing on the broad plain in his white, blood-spattered shirt, I saw a crown upon his blond head. He will become king over Israel." "You dare not say that, you are heir to the throne." A gesture of rejection. A smile. "I have seen it. It will be so." "And you?" "I will be long dead by then, or a priest, a scribe, or quite simply the brother of the queen." Then he continues quickly: "At that moment I thought only of the two of you, that the way was now clear for you to become man and wife. Father has promised a daughter to the one who vanquished the giant."

He embraces me, closes his eyes, and sleeps.

The way was not clear. Sick people like Saul are not to be trusted. The war came to a victorious end, the Philistines fled or were cut down by our men. I did not understand why I could not rejoice along with the others.

When I saw David again, he was still wearing the white shirt that had been spattered with blood over and over again. Jonathan took off his tunic and gave it to his friend, and his neck armor, his sword, and his bow as well. I never saw David in white again. He had become a warrior.

Saul made him his weapons bearer and gave him command over a thousand. But when Father got one of his attacks— they were increasing in number and severity—David took up his harp and sang. And he always succeeded in calming Saul's disturbed mind.

Whenever David took to the field with his men because enemies were threatening our borders, he was victorious. The people looked upon him as invulnerable. He always fought at the very front, but he never killed an opponent with his own hands. A miracle.

Our people love victors, love miracles. And because he was young and beautiful, they idolized him.

For our love he no longer had any time. He was always occupied, people sought his advice, it almost seemed as if he were granting audiences and the nights he spent with his soldiers, of whom Joab, a nephew of almost the same age, was the closest. We met in dark passageways, in corners of the palace hidden from view, embraced each other, kissed each other, he bit my lips bloody, hastily, breathlessly, without satisfaction. Whispered to each other that it would soon be different when we were finally man and wife.

But my father seems to have forgotten his promise. Could I talk with him? I know that there are fathers with whom that is possible. Mine is not one of them. Never has he said an unkind word to me. And yet I fear him. Fear his astonishment if I uttered my own thoughts.

It is Jonathan who reminds Father of his promise. "Did I say that?" asks Saul with the vacant look that he often has now. "Then it must be so. Therefore: Merab will marry David." Merab wails: "I? I am promised to Adriel. I want him."

Everything inside me tightens up. We are standing around the throne on which Saul is seated, the huge turban on his head, his mouth curled obstinately, as much as to say: no contradiction. I look at David. He is holding his harp in his arm, fingers the strings indolently, and sounds an almost celestial chord. Looks Saul full in the face: "Who am I to become the son-in-law of my lord and king? A shepherd, a singer, a warrior. And that I wish to remain." It sounds modest, is doubtless meant to sound modest, too, but I know him well enough to sense insolence. He is so sure of his ground already that he is toying with the king. But why has he not said that he does not want Merab, that he wants me? And suddenly I understand: he would even take Merab in order to become that which he claims he does not want to become.

A hand upon my shoulder. Jonathan whispers: "Have patience."

We leave Saul without another word having been said about David and Merab. She looks through him as if he were air.

"That cow," he says during our next embrace, "that conceited cow. If I marry her, you will simply become my second wife. Jacob loved Rachel, not Lea." "Fourteen years Rachel waited for Jacob." "And you would do that, Michal, wouldn't you?" "I cannot do that," I sob, "neither of us can." "No," he says laughingly, "that we cannot and will not do. Have faith in Jahwe."

I was unsuspecting, did not know what was facing me. Also did not know how much a person can bear.

A woman in the land of Canaan. The daughter of a king. Something for men to barter. The more important the men, the worse it is for the woman.

Are Merab and David betrothed? Are they not? No one knows. Even Mother does not dare to ask Saul about it. He does not bring it up again. His condition worsens. His roaring echoes through the palace. One day, while David is making music for him, Father screams out and hurls his spear at him. My nimble darling ducks, jumps aside and escapes. Takes refuge among us women.

We run to Father. He is lying on the floor screaming, rolling around, tearing his clothing, has foam around his mouth and howls that he finally knows now who wants to rob him of his throne, the love of his people and our love. He rears up, this tall man, and shakes his clenched fists at heaven: "He has bribed Jahwe." Then he lies motionless.

The hastily summoned physicians put compresses on his chest and force him to drink a potion. Like an infant, he spits part of it out again, then falls asleep. Leaden quiet in the room. Then David comes back. He weeps, says he wants to return to Bethlehem to herd his father's sheep again.

•

He meant it honestly in that hour, but he gives in to my urging and, probably even more, to Jonathan's, and stays. Plays for Saul again. He allows it, but shows his mistrust. Shows, that he wants to be rid of him. Be rid of—amounts to a sentence of death.

I laugh no more, eat nothing, grow thin. Am conscious every moment of the danger in which David now lives. Regret that I have persuaded him to stay. I often think of taking my life, when I ask him whether we should not do it together, he laughs at me: "Because of a crazy man? Throw away a life that is just beginning? No. It will be splendid, you will soon see. For you and for me."

I think of Jonathan's vision of the crowned David. But that is no comfort, rather, a burden. And I remain silent.

Father now looks like an old man who is no longer master of his limbs and no longer master of his mind. Often he searches for words, his gait is shuffling, many times saliva runs out of his mouth.

Suddenly he gives the order to prepare for the wedding of Merab and Adriel, a prosperous young man who can pay a high bride price. David is not mentioned again.

A glimmer of hope. I can laugh timidly again and begin to eat.

We are sitting around the great table. Then Jonathan says: "Father, Michal loves David. Give her to him as his wife." My brother has not prepared me for this bold move. It takes my breath away. "So," answers Saul distractedly, "Michal loves David. My little Michal. Just look at him. The shepherd who just turned up." "Whose music does you good," says Jonathan. He could have said: who slew Goliath. Who freed us from the Philistines. He does not say that. Says nothing that might strengthen Saul's delusions. David has become pale. Wants to be allowed to leave. Jonathan holds him back with a glance. "Do you want her, shepherd?" asks Saul without looking at David. A cattle merchant at market. If you want to buy the cow, that's fine, if not, that's fine, too. David says with restraint: "I love Michal, but I am a poor and lowly man. With what shall I pay the bride price?" Father smiles. Like a block of stone the smile closes out my happiness. Saul knits his brow, has a puffy, sly face. "I do not want a bride price from my musician. It suffices if he brings me the foreskins of a hundred Philistines." He is using me as a noose that is to tighten around David's neck. I perceive my own scream as if another had uttered it. No one pays attention to it. Let the women scream. Their way of meddling in the affairs of men.

David bows with the grace that is his: "As my king commands."

I cannot prevent him from marching out at the head of his troop of a thousand men. "He will return," says Jonathan. "Jahwe is with him." I see in his disturbed face that he is not so sure. "Jahwe is with him," I repeat despairingly and no longer believe that there is a Jahwe.

I do not take the foreskins literally. A figure of speech. But I will not be bought by David with a hundred slain Philistines. With the tears of a hundred weeping women. I do not want to be bought at all.

My poor flayed love. And the feeling that I have missed the moment to keep from having myself bought.

•

He returns. After just a few days. It is evening, we are sitting, as we do most of the time now, around Saul's throne, which he hardly leaves anymore, as if another might quickly sit on it in his absence. The oil lamps have been lighted, in the fireplace fragrant cedar wood is burning. David goes quickly up to Saul, two of his men drag in a basket, set it down. "My king," he says with a strange voice, "I bring the bride price. Not a hundred, that strikes me as really too little for a king's daughter, but two hundred Philistine foreskins." He opens the basket and, counting loudly, begins to take out one blood-smeared penis after the other and set them down in front of the throne.

I wish I would faint, but I would not even object to falling over dead. But I do not faint, nor do I die, not visibly to the others, but within me everything that I have been dies at this moment. I hear David counting on and on with his new voice: ". . . seventy-four, seventy-five, seventy-six . . ." Then my stomach churns, I have vomit in my mouth, run out, down the stairs, stand in front of the palace, spit out until finally all I retch up is an acidy fluid. Think: were they still alive when their penises were cut off, want to know and do not want to know, and am certain that I will never find out. Exhausted I lean against the wall. Then I see Jonathan beside me. He wants to put his arm around my shoulder, I gasp: "Do not touch me." He lets his arm fall. Mutely we remain standing beside one another in the deep twilight. When it has become quite dark and I shiver in the freshening night wind, he says softly: "Come along in." He takes me as far as my rooms. He leaves me without a goodbye.

The following day I am wedded to the one whom I have so very much wished for myself. Two blood-stained children, we stand before the altar. I, richly adorned with my mother's bridal jewelry of sapphires, emeralds, and diamonds, a veil held together by a golden crescent moon over my hair and face. We repeat the words of the priest, I as if in a dream, in an evil dream. They are the words—David wished it so—which, according to tradition, his ancestor Ruth had once spoken, the most ardent oath of faithfulness, not from a man to a woman, nor from a woman to a man, but from a young widow to the mother of her dead husband, from a woman from a foreign land to his people, his God:

> Entreat me not to leave thee,
> Nor to turn back from following thee.
> For whither thou goest, I will go also,
> And where thou dwellest, I will dwell with thee.
> Thy people are my people
> and thy God is my God.
> Where thou diest I will die.
> And there will I be buried.

Oh, if I could weep. Tearless, I stare through the mesh of my veil, the bars of my prison, in which I am confined for my lifetime.

The priest speaks, I do not listen. Why have I not run away? It was too late. Too late for everything. Even for dying. I had sworn to be faithful to David and one such as I is not capable of breaking her oath. I remained true to him as long as he lived, here, where he died, I want to die, whether I will be buried here as well is not in my power.

Yet I, who have never learned to lie, have lied during the ceremony. Less and less was his god mine as well. And when I realized with horror that, despite everything that had happened and continued to happen, I could not stop loving David, when I began to hate myself because of this love, the rejection of this God who was constantly becoming more cruel came to my aid and kept me from turning back. As long as I was successful I was a self-sufficient human being, not just David's creature. Do women have it easier among peoples who know not only gods but goddesses as well? With us it is difficult to be a woman, devastating to be a childless woman.

My father has given me a house as a wedding present, on the edge of Gibeah. We move in on the evening of our wedding day, the marriage bed stands ready and puffed up. When the maids have taken away my jewelry and veil and have departed after undressing me down to the shirt of soft linen, I lie down. How happy I could have been, how humiliated I am. Softly David enters, a small knife in his hand. Says laughingly that he must cut my finger, so that, according to tradition, he can throw a bloody cloth out of the window as a sign of the consummated marriage. "Give it here," I say, cut my thumb deeply and let the blood drop on a cloth that he holds out to me.

He lies down next to me, embraces and kisses me, I permit it without feeling, a wife must serve her husband, I have heard that since I was a little girl, that is deep-seated, but when he wants to penetrate me with his member, I see the blood-smeared penises again, revulsion seizes me, despair, and I thrust him away.

He does not understand, wants to take me by force, does not succeed, I have immense strength tonight. At first he tries lovingly, then he becomes enraged, strikes me, scratches me, chokes me. Finally he leaves me alone, throws the bloody cloth out the window, laughing loudly, murmured approval drifts up from those waiting down below. Lies, deceit; and I begin to cry uncontrollably. He fetches his shepherd's flute and plays. If he had not taken the knife away from me I would try to kill myself, perhaps him, too, I do not know.

The music stops, he lies down beside me and now he is crying too. I stop crying, stroke and comfort him as a mother does her child, tell him that I love him, sometime my revulsion will pass, I am sure of that. "David, my dearest, have patience, give me time, I will give you a son who is blond like you, dark-eyed like I am, a great singer, a prince to whom people will bow because he has brought them peace." He is no longer weeping. "Why do you say a prince? I am a singer and a warrior, and my son will also be a singer and a warrior." "You, David, will be king over Israel."

What am I saying? What have I done? Betrayed Jonathan. I could scream, my words hurt me so much, but some sort of strength—Jahwe? Not Jahwe?—makes me believe in them. I, too, see David with a crown, he will wear it, the shepherd boy, the harp and flute player, the unsullied one who kills no man, but cuts the penises off two hundred men or has them cut off.

Perhaps I led him to the thought for the first time that night, perhaps it had been slumbering in him for a long time and now suddenly awakened, perhaps he had already dreamed of being king while he was still watching over his father's sheep. Later he spread the legend that he had already been anointed by Samuel at home in Bethlehem, Jahwe's chosen one from the very beginning. But he had actually told me he did not know Samuel. A magician he was, who could bewitch people into seeing him just as he wanted to be seen. How was I to go on living at the side of a man whom I loved and who concealed himself from me because I saw through him? Everyone thought I was happy in the following weeks, except for Jonathan. His sorrow was like mine. He, too, loved a David who was becoming more and more a stranger to him.

Mother looked at me searchingly from time to time. Did she sense that things were not at their best between David and me? But when she asked me over and over: Nothing yet? I realized that she was only concerned about my becoming pregnant as quickly as possible. It appeared shameful to her to have a barren daughter.

I had hoped to become freer through my marriage, and remained as hemmed in as ever before. Walls everywhere. The duty of bearing children. New warriors. The more, the better. The individual does not matter, the people must survive. Jahwe's people. As long as his people lives, He lives, too.

David was often absent those days, there was no big war, but many little ones. Each time he returned a victor, his popularity grew and grew. Cries of rejoicing wherever he went, and, more and more often, the sing-song of the women: Saul has struck down his thousands. But David his myriads. An insult to the king. Saul appears not to have heard it. His condition had improved, yet I did not trust appearances. Old Eleazar said I was right, we should not deceive ourselves, the improvement would be of short duration, at the smallest instigation the sickness could break out again.

I went often to Eleazar, I trusted him. He took me and my troubles seriously. "Now you are disgusted," he explained, "time will heal. But you must talk about it with David."

I tried again and again. In vain. David did not understand me. Considered me a prude and thought I just needed to lie down and let him into me, he would put up with the fact that I had no desire, what mattered to him was the child. Our child, he said gently, your prince. But even this dream that had originated in the despair of the wedding night had passed. Then he became angry and cursed: "Your damned father, that fool who wanted the foreskins and I, the fool who brought them to him."

I said: I cannot and he said: you can. Tried to break me with harshness. I could not be broken because I had already been broken. He did not see that. He did not see anything any longer that lay beyond his world. And it was narrow: no world, but a road that led straight to power. Of the labyrinth he would have to go through before becoming king, he had no inkling.

People looked at us with pleasure, whispered to each other: how young and beautiful those two are. Well yes, we were beautiful. Each one alone, but even more so together. He so blond, I so dark. My body not yet disfigured by a child in my belly.

The day when Saul begins to rave again. When David is called and plays the harp. When he calms Father for a short time. When Saul throws his spear at him for the second time.

And again David succeeds in fleeing. He comes home, drenched in sweat, gasping for breath. "He will kill me. Wherever I go, he will find me and kill me." Then I hear the clanking of weapons in front of the house. I look out, there they stand, the king's soldiers, and want to get in. I call to them that David is sick, very sick, they should go away. To my astonishment, they obey, but leave two sentries behind. I am very calm now, stony hard, burned out, but know that I must use my powers of reason, since David has obviously lost his. "You must leave," I say, my voice sounds hard, "I will knot some pieces of cloth together and let you out a back window, the soldiers are standing only in front." Quickly I tie up bread and olives in a shawl, knot the sheets together. One end he ties around his waist. For one moment I lose composure. "I want to come with you, we belong together." "That would not be good, you would be an additional danger. But we will see each other again. In a few days I will let you know where I am. Then you can follow me." We embrace and kiss more tenderly than we had since our first night together. He stands on the windowsill, I let him down to a projecting wall, from which he can reach the neighbor's roof and the city wall. He unties himself. Slips away, catlike. A slender shadow. Israel's future splendor.

I pull the sheets up, undo them from one another. Suddenly I become dizzy, I lie down on the floor, my body jerks. "We will see each other again," I whisper, "soon."

We saw each other again, after many years.

To HAVE to flee, away from home, from everything that is familiar and habitual.

I, Grete, the late-born, had to flee, too, away from Germany, but we didn't flee far enough, only to Holland, and there our enemies caught up with us. They arrested Waiki, my beloved, took him away to the concentration camp at Mauthausen, where they murdered him.

That is long, long ago. A young woman experienced the persecution, an old woman is writing this down.

My husband was murdered, Michal's husband got away by a hair's breadth.

Three thousand years lie between us. A sufficient time for insight, but not much has changed.

Now I knew that I was a Jew. Only a Jew. Day and night, night and day. One to be destroyed, one trying to survive. Survival: the single form of resistance left to me.

Jew as a status. I had four Jewish grandparents, that counted.
My language and my culture were German, that didn't count.
Religion had never played a role for me. My ancient homeland
was Greece and its myths. Zeus and Apollo more important
than Jahwe. The rebel Antigone a shadow that accompanied
me at all times.

Beside her, David became unimportant.

Will to live and longing for death, depression and hope that
flared up. Belief in the Allied victory, in our victory, which we,
sentimentally and mistakenly, called the victory of the good.
Luckily we did not know how uncertain it was. Nor how
threadbare when it finally came. Evil destroyed, banished from
the world. Eternal peace. Shalom, shalom.

In the last weeks of the war I ran away from my hiding
place, I could no longer bear being penned up with two people
on whom I was dependent, found refuge with a friend who
herself was in hiding in a big room in an old patrician house.

In front of the room there was a garden with a blooming
magnolia in it. I walked around and around it, stroked it,
kissed it. The blossoms were, for me, a promise of things to
come. Shalom.

But from day to day the wish becomes stronger: I want to
go back to Germany.

I kept quiet about my plans. All around me was hate. Hate
that I could understand, that I could not share. Perhaps my not
hating was Jewish (if there even is such a thing).

Jews preserve life, do not destroy it. So I thought in the last
winter of the war.

My magnolia had just about lost its blossoms when the end
came. I was standing alone in the garden. Low, in formations
of threes, the American airplanes roared by above me. They

had been assured by the high command of the Wehrmacht that they would not be shot at while dropping food for the starving populace. There it was, life, long-stagnant blood began to flow. If I had been able to pray, I would have prayed then. I just said quite softly into the droning of the motors: "I don't want to hear the word Jew anymore."

～ *I*, MICHAL, lying on the floor, senseless from pain, slowly come back to earth. The danger is not yet past, I must deceive the king's henchmen, win time, increase David's lead. I get up awkwardly, stagger a little, then, from the pieces of fabric that my mother gave me as a wedding present, I pick out one that has the color of suntanned skin, crumple it together at one end, and lay it on David's bed so that this puffed up end looks out from the covers, push it around until it more or less has the shape of a head, lay blond goat hair on it, and push three pieces of charred wood into the face for eyes and mouth. From a little distance it could be taken for a sleeping person. I wait, without knowing for what, my heart pounds.

Loud knocking on the door, I go down, open it, three armed men are standing outside, one, their leader, asks for David. "David? He is sick, very sick. What do you want with him?"

"The king sends us." "And what does the king want of David? It is impossible for him to get up now and play for him." "I do not believe that the king has sent us to bring David to play for him. Nor do I believe that he is sick. I want to see him." "As you will." I go ahead, open the door, stand in the doorway so that they cannot walk into the room, and point to David's bed. They look over my shoulder and one mumbles scornfully, "More likely drunk than a fever." But they turn to leave, go, I bolt the door, lean against it, and now notice for the first time that my knees are shaking. How unworthy all of this.

I think of David so passionately, so full of longing that I am convinced I could live with him as a normal wife. In a few days, he said, I will surely be able to bear it a few days more.

Then the pain that it is my father who wants to kill David, my father, once loved and admired by me. Of whom I am a part. The same eyes. The same nose. The same way of raising my brows in astonishment. Often the same impatience. O Jahwe, bring it to pass that my mind does not become confused, too, that I may always know what I am doing and why I am doing it. That I am not forced to do harm to any man. That I am able to love, as long as I live.

It was my last prayer. In my despair I called upon Jahwe again. Although even then I no longer believed in a god who can grant the wishes of men. Who is He? What is He? A force from which we have sprung, into which we will return? That we do not know, that does not know us. We have called it Jahwe. We, a nomad people without land, kept in Egypt as slaves for a long time, until Moses led us away from there and we finally came here after years of wandering aimlessly, to the land that was promised to us. Promised by whom? My people say by

Jahwe, but why? Why promised just to us? The simple explanation: in Egypt, which then ruled Canaan, we presumably learned of this land in which it was claimed that milk and honey flowed. That is not so, the ground is hard and stony, but necessity taught us to cultivate it and we could bring in a harvest. It was not be to foreseen that when we came here, we would find that there were already other inhabitants: Amorites, Edomites, Moabites, Hittites in the interior, and, on the coast, the Philistines. We had to conquer them all, in part even exterminate them, in order to gain a foothold. Even our children learn that there was no other way to do it. I could never really see that, with a little effort we could have been able to live in peace with one another. But perhaps the country is really too small to nourish us all. But why announce with every new war, with every homicide, that it happened by Jahwe's command?

Part of that for which I prayed on the night when David took flight came to pass. Probably I had prayed only for things that I believed could be granted to me. My mind has remained sound, and I can still love. Or rather: I could love if there were someone here to love. Those closest to me are dead: Jonathan, David, Palti, and Absalom. Yes, really, all men. I like women, but there were and are none who took possession of me as these four. I like my little Egyptian maidservant Sulamith, who came to us with Solomon's wife, the Pharaoh's daughter, and was given to me as a servant. She has ash-colored hair, is pleasant, and sings me songs full of longing and lament that touch me like David's songs once did. And I harbor maternal feelings for Abishag the Shunammite, the beautiful and unhappy maiden whom Bathsheba put into David's bed to warm the old man who was constantly cold. Things were done without asking her, otherwise she could have said or screamed out that she loved Adonijah, the second-oldest son of David, and was loved by him in return. But this dream was over as soon as David had touched her—touched how much is his and her secret. Our laws are strict—whoever sleeps with a concubine of the king shows that he too lays claim to the throne. And that Solomon, who feared Adonijah as it was, could not allow—he did not hesitate long before having his half-brother murdered.

The henchmen come back again. "Orders of King Saul. If David is too sick to come to him on foot, he is to be carried there." "Why?" "That I do not know." They shove me aside, rush up the steps, angry cries are heard from above.

They come down with ominously slow steps. Stony faces. Odor of men. I am half faint with fear. Will they do me in? Their leader winds my hair around his hand, then strikes me in the face, twice, so that blood runs out of my nose. With a cord, they bind my hands behind my back and drag me through the dark and empty streets to the palace and up to the throne room.

There the king, my father, is waiting with my four brothers. He looks at me. Startled, a blood-smeared daughter with a black eye is not a pretty sight, then he bellows: "Why did you let him escape?" I want to say that I helped David take flight because I love him, then I see that Jonathan has put a finger to his lips and is shaking his head ever so slightly. "He threatened to kill me if I did not help him flee," I say quickly. Father strikes his spear on the floor angrily and says: "I will catch him soon, then he will atone for hurting you so, my poor child." He believes that David has hit me so that I bled. I do not contradict him and am allowed to go. To my empty house, in which there are no longer even my dolls. On the floor lies a piece of frayed cloth.

At that time, I had not yet learned how to put up with pain. It had not yet become part of me. Every night I lay sobbing in David's bed and now it no longer seemed so certain to me that I could follow him.

The endless days of waiting, when nothing happens. No news. Nothing. Slowly all hope dies.

My only support is Jonathan, my tall brother, the honorable one. He comes every day to comfort me. But there are the long, lonely nights and sleep is much too short. And every morning a blow to the heart: David is gone. Where is he? In Bethlehem with his father and brothers? No, Saul would look for him there first. I do not know where I should send my thoughts. Suddenly I realize! David is running away to a place where there is power. To Samuel. It hurts me to think of that old man whom I fear. The kingmaker. Who put Saul on the throne. Will he do the same with David? For myself, I do not wish David to become king. Yet he himself surely wishes it. And because I love him, more and more each day, there is nothing left for me but to wish for what he wants.

A wife must remain silent. Subordinate herself to her husband. Will it ever be otherwise? Will the day come when a woman is not sold by her father, does not have to be one among many in the house of her husband?

Once I learn from Jonathan: David has been here. Secretly, he has come back from Samuel's dwelling at Ramah, to try again to win Saul's favor. In vain. Jonathan has begged for mercy for him. Then Father became even more enraged, pointed his spear at Jonathan. But he did not throw the spear. The fear of David is deep-seated, unbearable for Saul is the thought that his own son is siding with David. David is gone again without having seen me. Where, Jonathan does not know. But he has been charged with telling me that David will not forget me and will send for me one day. I am not made for the life he is now facing. I must have patience and wait. What does David know of me? Not how tough I am, what I could endure, if it were demanded. Not even how very much I love him.

"The life of a fugitive is hard," says Jonathan, "perhaps he will have to rob and murder in order to survive."

He became a robber, but he did not murder. His hands— unstained by blood. He first became a murderer as king. Even then he did not do it himself, gave a sign to his warriors and they obeyed. Many times they were quicker than his wishes. If I myself had not heard his command to spare Absalom, I could not have lived longer. Do I want to live?

Beside me the little dagger that Palti gave me on parting. A quick thrust into my heart, it would have peace. Or cut my arteries. But then a maid would find me before I was dead. Summon the king's physician, Eleazar's son, who is different from his father, frivolous, spoiled, with a large harem. Arteries can be bound up and sewn. So not much to be said for replacing one fear with another. I must go on living. An old woman, plagued by memories, yet during all the unhappiness through which I have come, something shines out now and again: Jonathan's love, David's early passion, Palti's loyalty, and Absalom's admiration. When he said you are the smartest, mother, you are the dearest. My mother who was my wife in an earlier life. There is no earlier life, Absalom. Then he laughed: who knows? He liked David's constant appeals to Jahwe as little as I did.

⟨⟩ DURING the time when David had to hide from Saul, I, Michal, began to think. Naturally, I had thought earlier, too, but what I did now was different, entirely different. I regarded the world critically. No longer unquestioningly took that which was told to me as true. Each one of us acted as tradition prescribed. Everything seemed to me to be congealed, nothing fluid.

My father was the king and my mother the wife of the king. What they did was determined by their rank. Without it they would be immobilized, incapable of moving, incapable of acting. How did they know what morals and propriety were? What was the "normal" that mother liked to invoke so much, toward which she behaved as David did toward Jahwe, reverently, trustingly? What was it? To kill human beings seemed to me to be the height of abnormality. Even though most people found that quite in order. Does the norm arise from the opinion of the majority? Was murdering, if most people were followers of a murderer, normal? I wanted to live according to my own law.

Jonathan had told me of a Greek maiden, a king's daughter like myself—she was called Antigone; he had heard the story from a Hellenic slave. The maiden's brothers had killed each other in a duel for supremacy over the city in which they had grown up.

The "good one"—but why good?—was the one who had lived in the city and had been chosen as the future king by his uncle who was acting as regent; he was to be buried with all honor. The body of the "bad" one—why bad?—was to be thrown out and devoured by wild beasts. Anyone who buried him would be put to death. Now, however, it was exactly this one whom his sister loved above all others. And she buried him. She cast a handful of earth on the guarded corpse, was seized and walled up in a rocky grave because she had followed her own law, loyalty to her brother, and not the arbitrary law of her uncle. I admired this Greek maiden very much, wanted to be like her, yet knew that I was too weak.

If there had not been a David, I would have been braver. My courage was crippled by my love. It, the most precious thing that I possessed, had to be protected. I had to preserve myself, the vessel of this love, beside which everything else could perish. So egotistical.

I arise, wash, dress myself, I play a little on the harp that David gave me. One day like the next. No husband, no child.

So young, so useless. I had always laughed at the old widows who refused to get up and spent the whole day in their beds. Now I myself am exactly like them. Completely superfluous, do not need to worry about anyone. Call my maid who brushes my hair. That feels good. Do not stop yet, Rachel. I envy you, because you can work, probably you envy me because I am a princess. To be a princess only means to be an especially dear and precious ware, believe me, Rachel. He who loved me had to pay the most loathsome bride price. If I had been an ordinary maiden, my father would have accepted with pleasure a few sheep from David's father. But why pay at all?

Why is a wife a commodity? Keep on brushing, Rachel, do not stop.

Now Jonathan comes, I send Rachel away.

Throw myself into his arms, am happy for a moment. This brother may love me without paying. He is downcast, has shadows under his eyes, sits down, pulls me down beside him on the couch of animal skins. Puts his arm around my shoulder: "Michal," he says softly, "eventually you would have to hear it: David has married again."

It is the custom in our country that a man has several wives, the greater the power, the renown of the man, the greater the number of his wives. I had always reckoned on having another one beside me, a third, and perhaps even a fourth, but beside me. Now there is one without me, perhaps she does not even know that I exist, that I am his first wife. "Who is she?" I ask weakly. "Abigail, the widow of a very rich man named Nabal. David and his men offered him protection without being asked, if he would give them enough supplies. Nabal refused the payment. Then Abigail, who they say is young and beautiful, packed the supplies on mules and took them to David. "And they fell in love?" Jonathan nods.

"In any case he assured her that she had prevented him from killing, because he was about to do away with Nabal and his men." "You know how much importance David places upon his clean hands. On the following day Jahwe showed some consideration, Nabal took sick. After ten days he died. Abigail nursed him devotedly. David cursed everyone who thought ill of it. A week later she was his wife."

A murderess, I think, and everything in me contracts, he loves a murderess, to her belongs his passion. For her, now, his song.

I did think ill of it. Will David's curse strike me? I believe in the power of such curses.

When I return to David after years, Abigail becomes my friend. Her joyfulness, her warmth, her beauty are irresistible. Immediately she vacates the place of the first wife to me. There are already several and a number of concubines besides. Abigail laughs my cares away, a sister whom I can trust. I love her round brown eyes, her dark blond hair that sits like a crown on her head, her skin that is tinted brown by the sun, that smells like new-mown hay and warm earth. A murderess? I did not believe it and do not believe it even today, more likely a child of good fortune. Nabal, her unloved husband, that ugly, uncouth man, that bloodsucker, a drunkard, a glutton, forced on her by her parents, dies at the very moment when the one who is to be loved comes into her life. Jahwe? Oh, Jahwe.

She took me in her arms when I was sad. David loved to look at her. She was still beautiful, a few years older than he and I, but physical love was past, there were other, younger dalliances for David before Bathsheba came. Abigail laughed: Such is life, Michal, we must be happy if the love of such a man belongs to us for a short span of time.

A March day spun from silk, a day for being happy. Happy? No. But calmer. I know now that David lives. Scanty the news that Jonathan brings me. He does not tell where he heard it and I do not even ask.

David has been at Nob, the place of priests, and has let himself be given consecrated bread and the sword of Goliath, that had been kept there, by Ahimelech the Highest of the Priests. Oh, what, let it be given, he swindled it out of them, said that he was on a secret mission for King Saul.

"Doeg saw him there, that is not good," says my brother dejectedly. Doeg, the Edomite, just recently the king's favorite and weapons bearer, a cold, suave officer, who takes advantage of Father's helplessness. "He will tell about it?" "On that you can depend."

Now David is said to be in the wilderness of Ziph and gathering about him a troop of loyal and dedicated men. His brothers are there too, his nephew Joab, son of his sister Zeruiah, and many young men for whom things have become too confining at home.

When Jonathan has gone, I take David's harp and pick out some chords for myself, but none resembles the celestial ones he conjures up, even when he just playfully plucks the strings. I sing a bit, too, my voice does not sound bad, even David once said that he liked to listen to me.

Once I believe I hear cries, the death cries of men or animals. It must be an illusion, profound peace reigns at the moment. When slaughtering is done, it takes place far away from the city.

Aimlessly I walk through the rooms and listen. It is completely quiet now, but the soft scratching at the door is not a noise of my imagination. I open it, before me stands an unfamiliar, teenage boy in a shirt that has been spattered over and over with blood. His thin face is wet with tears. He is Abiathar, he says, son of the High Priest Ahimelech, not yet a priest himself, but a pupil of his father's. He stammers: "Jonathan said: run to David's house. Tell my sister Michal she should hide you until early tomorrow morning." It comes out haltingly. I take him in my arms, that is all I can do, take him upstairs, lay him on David's bed. Very, very slowly, interrupted by pauses that seem endless to me, I learn the horrible truth.

Saul bade all the Priests of Nob, sixty-five in number, come to Gibeah and commanded the soldiers on guard to kill them. The latter, simple men of the people, refused to lay hands on Jahwe's Priests. Then Doeg came, Doeg all alone, and cut down the unarmed men with his sword. "All?" I ask in disbelief. "All. My father last of all." I understand, understand only too well. The massacre was the punishment for Ahimelech's helping David. David is the enemy, Saul's only goal: to destroy David, then no one can steal the throne from him.

I am as weak as the weeping youngster: "He has spared you because you are not yet a priest?" "No, Jonathan pulled me away from the melee, out from between the corpses, he knew me from the time when he was studying religion in the house of my father."

Hatred grows within me. Hatred of my father, hatred of his helpers. Hatred of everyone who did not prevent him from the murders, hatred of Jahwe, hatred of myself. I do not believe that a person can hate without hating himself. This I learned on that night. I lie on the floor beside the bed. "Michal," implores the boy from above, "Michal, get up, I cannot bear it that I have brought sorrow to you."

But I remain lying there, cannot get up at all, it is like a spasm that paralyzes my limbs. Only once do I scream out: "Why does Jahwe permit this?"

"Nothing happens against his will," says Abiathar with deep conviction. "He is a stern and just God. Probably he wanted to punish us for something about us that has displeased him. We have failed to understand and carry out his plan. He has given, He has taken, praised be the name of the Lord."

I shudder at this faithfulness. If anyone is guilty, it is I. Why have I coveted David for my husband? Every misfortune began with that.

I think it, but do not say it. Amidst tears the night passes. In the morning comes Jonathan, clear, decisive. "You must go away, Abiathar. I will give you a guide who will take you to David. The only place where you are safe now. Tell David what has happened, it will strengthen his courage."

They leave. I watch them go, full of envy of Abiathar, who may go to David. Then I fetch a bucket of water, wash my hands for a long time with sand and bran, for hours. They are long since clean, yet I keep on washing.

Thus David obtained his High Priest Abiathar, one of the most loyal of men. Together with his king, he rose to prominence. That I had helped him on the night after the day of the murders, that he forgot.

At Saul's court nothing more was said about the murder of the priests. We were all cowardly. And since Jahwe did not punish, one could assume that he had nothing against the extermination of his priests. Nob was leveled after the murder, even the women and children had been struck down.

I, GRETE, the late-born, in a late world that is gradually being ruined, still very often heard the word "Jew," which I had not wanted to hear anymore after the war, used it myself, it had become a compulsion, a compulsion to profess the fact even then, when people didn't want to hear it at all.

As a Jew I had been persecuted, as a Jew, Waiki, my beloved, my husband, had been murdered. I couldn't put being Jewish aside, like a dress that had become old-fashioned.

Being Jewish is a fact, but I'm not successful in giving it any content. Not possible without belief in God.

I knew as much of history as any person who lived more or less privately, as much politics as I'd allow myself. Now and then a protest against atomic weapons and similar monstrosities, no more.

Tried to master old age, a difficult task that consists of renunciations, every day, every hour a new renunciation.

In my youth I had often considered it right to renounce something, without its being demanded, voluntarily. Now renunciation is forced from outside and hurts.

Colors have become dull, smells weaker, thinking is not as lively as it was just a short time ago. Tiredness limits my ambition. My train of thought comes apart, can't be put back together again, nothing more comes of it as it used to, when out of many good ideas came one very good one, in lucky moments: inspiration while writing.

I did what I had always wanted to do and had hardly ever done, wrote books, was finally a witness, and recognized late success with amazement, delight, and composure, more composure than if it had come earlier.

After a long time I had a dog again, a female Lhasa Apso, a little, black ball of wool with lively, intelligent eyes. I called her Shagi, for Abishag of Shunam, the beautiful maiden whom Bathsheba put into bed with a David who was old and constantly chilly, so that she could warm him, which, of course, never really succeeded. I was not chilly, but I, too, was old, consequently a dog had a similar function with me. Shagi was the favorite of everyone who saw her. With instinctive trustfulness she jumped up on everyone we met, as if she wanted to say: look how pretty I am.

For her first summer we were in Ticino, where there were no fences to limit her freedom of movement, but she never wandered far from home.

I was happy with the dog and repressed the fact that things were not going as well that summer as in all of the preceding ones, that it was harder for me to go uphill and short walks soon tired me.

But then it happened: I, the one who was always healthy, who had been able to depend on her body and its strength all the time, became ill.

A mild heart attack, followed by a stroke, put me down.

Hospital in Locarno. Very, very foreign. Unfriendly nurses, impersonal physicians. At first the intensive care unit, then a tiny single room with a high, narrow window, in front of which hangs a long, dark green curtain. When it is pulled up, I look out on the beautiful, dark roof of the Basilica of San Francesco. The smallness of the room is not disturbing, if I can just be alone.

And here I am. In my bed, in myself, locked in with my circular thoughts that can no longer be directed, as if in a prison cell from which there is no escaping. The only way out would likely be that leading to death; probably I'm not looking for it energetically enough, otherwise I'd soon find it.

My thoughts circle around: incessantly, boring in: "As if a mill wheel were going around in my head."

But my uncontrollable thoughts do not bring me any Goethe poems, only fragments of Schiller's ballads that I don't like; "The Hostage," with its unbelievably mild tyrant who lets the man who wanted to murder him go free for three days to attend his sister's wedding. Just what a tyrant would do. Besides that, this tyrant is naive, when he says: "I may thus be, if you grant my wish, the third member of your alliance." So simple. In the vernacular, it's called an "earworm"—words, bits of music that won't leave you alone. A pathetic male voice recites: "Back! You can no longer save your friend: Then save your own life." That's how deeply all this is engraved in my poor brain, which won't conjure up for me the Mozart music that I long for, but rather, hit songs from the twenties. The operetta tunes of Massary, Dietrich, Karlweis, Gründgens. Nostalgic longing for the time that was bold and daring, clever and often cynical, and which I experienced, just from the sidelines, for a few semesters as a student in Berlin. My phonograph records from those days, rescued from the war, are lying quite near here, upstairs in my little house.

Go away, just go away you ballads and songs.

My thoughts do not circle—what luck—around persecution, although a friend heard me say while in a coma: I have Auschwitz. (A quotation from one of my books.)

I'm unaware of the stroke that develops overnight. Not of the left-sided paralysis, not even that involving the left hand.

Not a moment's knowledge of the danger. Although everyone who saw me those days claims I was fighting desperately. Can you fight against an enemy you don't know anything about? Is the inclination to stay alive, not to glide over into a gentle death, so overwhelming? I am no longer here in the hospital, in this small room with the dark green curtain. I am on a mountain. Huge swarms of blackbirds pass by my window, that is not a dream, they're real.

During a previous illness, not one from within, a sedative overdose, I had believed that the intensive care unit located on the ground floor was up high and I thought I could feel a slight swaying of the bed. Whatever, it has to be up, high up, as far away as possible from people. So now the mountain. Here the barracks-like hospital buildings are standing in a large semicircle, I go into one of them, am standing in a hall with many doors to the right and left. I open one, lie down on the bed standing empty in the small room. Only after I am lying there do I notice that the call-bell is missing from the trapeze above me.

Feeling of abandonment, I cannot make myself be noticed. No one knows where I am. The simplest way out, just to get up again, does not occur to me. I'll starve. Yes, I'm hungry, mightily hungry. Surprised, angry, I realize that I have not eaten for days. Just wait, you'll see, I'll write a newspaper article about how badly patients are treated in your highly touted Swiss hospitals. This idea calms me a bit and I immediately start to compose the article in my head. I don't even know that I can't swallow, that the left side of my palate is paralyzed. Nobody tries to explain to me what's wrong.

Then I am fed through a nasogastric tube. When it is put in, it hurts, I resist, grab the hands of the young doctor and announce threateningly: I'll scream so that they even hear me in the street. Just calm yourself Madame, we're only doing what's necessary, says the doctor, shocked.

Since I don't see the necessity, I experience the procedure as a torture. I try to pull out the tube, then they tie my hands fast to the bed and the torture is complete.

Untie me, I beg every nurse who comes in and each one reacts the same way: *Il dottore ha detto no.*

How I hate them.

Finally a young female physician from northern Switzerland (mother tongue German, a woman among nothing but men) tells me the truth. That I had a stroke is a shock for me, different from a heart attack, a permanent impairment.

Who's going to take an author seriously whose brain was switched off for a while?

Keep quiet? But I don't want to keep quiet, can't do it. It is part of me to want to tell the truth, to have to.

From Locarno I go to a hospital in Upper Bavaria, where

everything is better. I understand the nurses and they understand me (it was not just a problem with the language, I did all right with Italian in Locarno). Am no longer a stranger, am no longer tortured. At home in Germany? Yes, at home in Germany.

Despite that, fears. None, or at least very few of death (there can be no Auschwitz in nothingness). But fear that it could start all over again, intensive care unit, nausea, total dependency, thinking that can no longer be directed.

Over and over again I imagine that I learned a trick while I was in coma, how to go on living without getting older. I've forgotten the trick. Many times, when I'm falling asleep, I hunt for it desperately.

Deep depression between hospitalization and going home. I'm sitting in a dark hole with smooth, icy walls (a crevice in a glacier), I can't get out now and probably never will.

Patience, people say, they all say it, that can't really be so difficult, with your energy.

Hardly anyone seems to know that energy is the first thing to be destroyed by sickness, that a sick person is also a weak person. Besides that, everyone has a grandmother or an aunt who got through similar problems. I come to the conclusion that they were all patient lambs in comparison to me, who wants to live and love the earth just as before.

Earlier, when I heard about an illness, I had often believed: that's bad, but I can't get it, not me.

Now I am convinced that I have every conceivable illness within me and that I will soon break out with all of them.

Then it's all over. I don't know: there is no sharp borderline between being sick and being healthy and that is perhaps the most difficult hurdle to get over on the way to recovery.

Thoughts can be controlled again. I am no longer an easy prey for hit songs and Schiller's ballads. "The Hostage" bothers me sometimes, can be wiped away, however, and, if I wish, replaced by a monologue from Faust. I can call up Goethe and Mozart (*Mann und Weib und Weib und Mann reichen an die Gottheit an,* instead of: I am head over heels in love), and it is possible for me to write again, now and then.

But I am dependent on the help of others, can't go shopping for myself, can't cook anymore, need another person for every chore. The worst thing is that I no longer may drive by myself, perhaps can't even do it, sickness and age have, I sense that myself, diminished my ability to react.

Need people who plague me with their advice, who want to direct my life for me: you have to do it this way, don't walk too long, better to do it more often than all at once. Lie down and take a nap after lunch, I would, it'd be better if, you're doing that the wrong way, don't be so nervous. Wonderful that you can at least write. No it is not wonderful, not a bit. It is an incredible strain. The constant fear of not being able to, anymore.

The illness has changed me (not transiently, even that is final), has made me aggressive and fearful.

People get on my nerves. Ever since, my relationships with them are diminishing and, because I sense that, it pushes me deeper into depression and rejection.

I am sitting at my desk in my pretty study. Have some pieces of metal sculpture by my sculptor friends in front of me and am looking at the filled bookcases alongside that signal security. In the window between the shelves stands a pot with bright pink azaleas and a vase with long-stemmed pink roses.

Somewhat perplexedly I think back: why did I get sick? Was it my ever-present feeling of guilt that I survived? Was it because I made the pain of persecution and sorrow over Waiki the theme of my writing? My knowing about Auschwitz and that I constantly dragged this knowledge around with me?

Have I strayed too far from my roots?

Do my figures hold it against me, that I, who know so little about the Bible, have undertaken to write about them?

Was it simply that my blood vessels are old and at a certain moment during a short walk in the mountains transported too little oxygen to my heart?

But why? For what reason?

Will the day come and, if it comes, when, on which I can say: the illness is behind me?

And David? And Michal? Will I be able to summon up enough strength and patience to tell their long, complicated, sad story to the end?

With the same quality as previously? Doubt, apprehension that I cannot get away from. Recognize the uncertain, accept, be alert, be honest, go on writing.

I, MICHAL, an old woman in Solomon's palace, shivering in the shade of the olive tree and yet knowing that, without this shade, I would not be able to stand it in the glaring sunlight: the wondrous star that maintains our lives and provides nourishment, that causes the grapes to ripen and imparts sweetness to them until they are pressed into intoxicating wine, takes the breath away from us old ones with its wildness. Anything, just no heat. Heat is something for young people. For hours I could sit in the sun's rays, they could not harm my dark skin, at most they colored it just a little darker. Indeed, when David had not yet been away for long, I sat on the flat roof of my house in the sun for many hours and days and thought about the world, about myself, and my solitary life.

Many times I implored my parents to help me, with my eyes, never with words, but they did not help me, only said:

that accursed one, that rabble-rouser and robber who makes our peaceful land unsafe with his band, has forfeited his life and you, our daughter, he has dishonored and deserted you, God shall punish him.

They did not say and probably had even forgotten that he had to flee because my father sought to kill him, him, who had freed us from the Philistines, who had defeated Goliath.

A deserted wife without a child, without a letter of divorce, the most miserable creature in the whole world. The monotony of these months, I believed it would last my whole life long. I imagined myself walled up while still alive.

Every day I went to the palace, listened to the quarrelsome talk of my mother, stood behind the wooden latticework of the window and watched the goings-on in the courtyard, the pushing and shoving of the supplicants who had come for an audience.

We are sitting around the table, Father pounds it with his fist, the pitchers rattle. He stands up, says to me: "Come along." Goes ahead with Jonathan, into the throne room where supplicants are waiting for him. Looks carefully at those who are drawn up in rank and file, finally beckons over to him a homely, actually ugly, young man with a large nose: "What is your name?" "Palti, my Lord, son of Laish." "Why are you here? Speak out loud and clear." "Qu-quarrel with our neighbor." Saul wrinkles his brow at the stuttering: "Can you not speak properly?" "Y-yes, I can." "What is the quarrel about?" "About th-three sh-she-asses." Saul's face softens, it is well known that he once set off to look for she-asses that had run away and came home with a kingdom. She-asses are pleasing to him. "Do they belong to you, the she-asses?"

"Yes, to us." "You are not poor?" "N-no, m-many sheep, c-cows, and two ca-camels." "So, two camels as well. That is a lot. Do you know that one, there?" he asks suddenly and points to me.

The stranger, of whom I now know that he is called Palti, looks at me, a bit frightened, but quickly stutters: "Mi-Michal, your daughter, David's wife." "David is no more. Do you want her? I will forgo the bride price for you. Tomorrow you can be married."

If my father had torn the clothing from my body it would not have been any different. I had the feeling that the ground was being pulled away from beneath my feat.

Is Father joking? No, he is not joking. I know his face with its empty, indifferent look.

"Take each other by the hand," he says. As if asleep, I stretch out my right hand to the stranger and he takes it in his, which is moist.

"Embrace each other!"

Then he, who does not dare to contradict the king, takes me tenderly in his arms and brushes his closed lips across my trembling mouth.

Whispers almost soundlessly: "I will re-respect you as Da-David's wife."

I experience everything as if it had nothing to do with me. A play is being put on, I just look on, see, also, how Jonathan reaches angrily for his sword.

On the following day we are married. Without ostentation, without bridal jewelry.

I am agitated, but not particularly sad. Anything that can free me from my lethargy, get me away from here, is agreeable to me, even this shy, ugly, yet sympathetic man.

That evening Palti takes me home to his simple house, in which I feel comfortable from the first moment on.

Thus began my second marriage, which became a good one, although it had nothing to do with physical love. Palti never forgot that I was David's wife, David's property. He who after a short time no longer stuttered, still did it only when he had to say David's name.

Instead of lamenting, I said yes to Palti.

My longing for David remained, for his beauty, his music, curiously enough, often more for his music than for himself.

Not even Jonathan understood my relationship to Palti. He held it to be a breach of faith against one still beloved by him. Even for him, the closest one, I was from then on: our poor Michal.

I could see that it was difficult for him to understand that I would inwardly give up David, the brilliant, the gifted one, Jahwe's angel, for an insignificant, shy man without any external merits. Palti was no hero. I had had enough of heroes. Palti was a Jew, such as I imagined a Jew ought to be: without warlike ambition, not vengeful, patient, compassionate, righteous, human, and gentle.

He tried to give me everything that I wanted, but I did not have many wishes, the one, piercing—David—he could not fulfill for me.

He knew that, too, gave me fabrics and brooches, I adorned myself—for whom? We were often amused, laughed, indeed laughed frequently. I do not believe that a person can live without laughing. We made little poems, one for the other, we celebrated, every day was a celebration. Not much happened without our being happy with one another. I was deeply convinced that nothing could part us other than death. Whenever Palti returned home from the fields in the evening, he would call out right away from the entrance: "Michal, my little Michal." Then he would kneel down before me and kiss the hem of my garment. Often he smelled of goats and sheep, it was soon a familiar smell.

One day Jonathan comes, gloomy, something must have happened. He tells us that David has become a vassal of King Achish of Gath, one of the kings of the Philistines and has received the city of Ziklag as a fiefdom. "Will he now fight against his own people?" asks my brother. "Never, Jonathan, never."

From this moment on, I am the only one who does not have doubts about David. I know his ambition and know that he would never fight against the people he wants one day to rule.

Even Jonathan, the faithful one, renounces him and does not understand me when I defend David and say: what else could he have done other than go to the Philistines?

Saul continued to pursue him relentlessly, possessed by the wish for revenge (revenge for something that lay in the future, that his sick mind foresaw). He was convinced that David would rob the throne from him. It did not come to pass. When David became king, rightful and chosen, our father, who had fought against a specter, was long since dead.

Once, in the wilderness of Ziph, King Saul came upon a cave in which he lay down to sleep. In the morning when he awakened he noticed that a tassel had been cut from his coat. He walked out of the cave in front of which stretched a ditch. On the other side of the ditch stood David, who waved the coat tassel and called: "Why do you persecute me, my Lord and

King, I have done nothing to you and will do nothing to you. You are the anointed of the Lord and I am your servant."

For a short while, Saul was moved by David's magnanimity, then fear seized him again, and he continued to pursue him.

Why did David spare Saul in the cave? Did he sense that this was a never-to-be-repeated opportunity to portray himself splendidly to his own people? He knew what his people loved: heroes who are noble to their enemies.

Never would he have laid a hand on an anointed one and shown his followers how one gets rid of a king. For, one day, he too would be king. Of that he was deeply convinced.

He had a goal and went toward it without deviating. He was a trickster, a magician, a conjuror who pulls live pigeons from a tightly knotted kerchief in the marketplace. Look, it would have been easy for me to kill Saul, he was in my hands, it is permitted to do away with a pursuer. Anyone else would have done it in my place. Not I, I am no murderer, my hands are clean and that they will remain until the day when you make me your king. I know that day will come and when it happens in good time, I will not be closed to your entreaties.

Hoofbeats in front of the house, I, Michal, look down. Jonathan is dismounting from his horse. It is the last time that I see him, but I do not know that. I never think that anything could happen to him, my strong and yet careful brother.

He reports that, in David's absence, the Amalekites have fallen upon Ziklag, laid waste the city, and carried off David's wives. Yes, there is already another besides, or actually before, Abigail, Ahinoam, a Jezreelite, the mother of his eldest son Amnon.

David was said to have set out after his enemies, was able to annihilate them, and free his wives.

.

The Philistines were gathering for a death blow against Israel. Achish wanted David to be with him. But the other Philistine kings did not trust him. (Probably rightly.) Thus he had to, was allowed to, remain at home.

It came to a great battle on Mount Gilboa, in which my Jonathan, the king, my father, and two of my other brothers were killed. It was said that Saul threw himself on his sword in order not to fall into the hands of the enemy. Palti reported it to me, yet I did not understand. It was the first time that death came so near, the first time that a person whom I loved did not return. This final "Never again" struck me cruelly, I lay upon my bed and wept for Jonathan.

For long hours I screamed his name, Palti stood beside me, tears ran down his face, he had liked Jonathan even though he knew that he, too, took a bit of my love away from him. In the morning, after awakening from an uneasy sleep, it was even worse. I tried to recall Jonathan's voice, I did not succeed, even the voice was gone and would never again say "little Michal."

Palti told how the enemies had nailed father's and Jonathan's bodies to the city gate at Beth-shan. This image tormented me without respite, I could not push it away for a moment. Jonathan with his arms stretched wide apart, one who could endure, he must have suffered horrible pain and I suffered with him, without considering that he no longer felt anything. Did he no longer feel anything? What was that: being dead? Was it that a person simply ceased to exist? No longer thought anything? No longer felt anything? Why did Jahwe let people die? A badly arranged world. Give me a torch so that I can set it on fire. It should burn, burn, it is not worth anything more.

I did not see Jonathan dead, but I saw him within me, his beloved face, formed by good thoughts, staring, his eyes unseeing, his mouth stretched taut. I did not see Jonathan. I saw death.

The men of Jabesh, the neighboring city to Beth-shan, took the bodies down from the gate, burned them, gathered up and buried their bones.

I mourned and Palti mourned with me. And another besides. David mourned also and composed a song of lament, which soon became famous:

> Mine is sorrow over you
> My brother Jonathan
> Closest of friends to me
> Wondrous was your love to me
> Passing the love of women.

The feeling of mourning together brought David nearer to me again. I knew he had loved Jonathan, as far as he could love at all. I also admired his courage, that he acknowledged this love before all the world.

Mother felt that he had besmirched the memory of Jonathan with the words: "wondrous was your love to me, passing the love of women," but she knew and understood nothing of her children. At the ceremony of mourning she had screamed and torn her garments. This was the custom and she always did what was the custom.

One can choose other friends, other loves, but not a brother.

My youth, when there was a brother, especially this brother, is past. Irreplaceable Jonathan. We needed no words, understood each other silently, knew every moment about things we had in common.

Deep under the earth, the sea, Sheol, the eternally dark kingdom of the dead, where they wander aimlessly and can nevermore return to the light.

Many times I dreamed, and still dream, of being there, then I wake up, my pillow is wet from tears and I do not know whether I long more for the darkness or for the light.

Added to our despair was the uncertainty as to where the victorious Philistines would turn next, whether they would fall upon us. We decided to flee. Some of our people were already breaking up their homes, Palti wanted to stay with his animals and I agreed. Senseless to rescue yourself, when all is lost.

I went over to Jonathan's house. There they were in the midst of packing up everything. Jonathan had a little son named Mephibosheth. The child looked like him, I loved him very much. A chambermaid was carrying Mephibosheth through the confusion that reigned in the house. She tripped over a chest that was lying around and let the child fall. He screamed and wailed and could not be quieted.

"My feet, oh, my feet, ow it hurts," he howled. I took him in my arms, covered his face—Jonathan's face—with kisses. Then I tore myself away from the last piece of him.

Mephibosheth's feet never got well, they remained crippled throughout his life. David later took him into his house in Yerushalayim, treated him as one of his own sons, and the people admired him for that too. Whatever David did, nothing was held against him. The people persisted in the belief: as long as we follow him, nothing can happen to us.

It would have been so easy to see the stains that dulled his splendor. Only shortly before his death did the people turn away from him and no longer wanted to follow him into the great war that he was planning. In order finally to destroy all the enemies of Israel.

I have never helped David to increase his fame. Bathsheba did that, she was ambitious for him, for herself, and, most of all, for her son Solomon.

I was not a good queen. Too great was my horror at that which a king like Saul could bring to pass.

David was more gifted, bolder than most. Yet I do not believe that the highly gifted, bold, ambitious ones are good fortune for the world.

WHENEVER I, old Michal, ancient Michal, think back to the time after Jonathan's death, I am still filled with horror. Did I already know then, from the very beginning, what his death meant for me? Beyond the pain of the moment, against which I tried to hurl myself as long as my grief had not yet blended into the all-encompassing lethargy in which I persisted listlessly and devoid of thought, as if I were waiting for something to happen? Naturally nothing happened, or at least nothing that could have helped me. Palti was a comfort, yes, naturally, but the person who had always watched over me everywhere and who had built up a barrier between me and eternity, Jonathan, was no longer there. I was a sister, can anyone imagine how dreadful it is to be a brotherless sister? Jonathan had done more to shape me, to leave an imprint upon me, than David or Palti. I was no lover, no wife, and no mother, no matter how much pleasure I had at playing mother to Absalom, I was and remained a sister and did not wish to be anything else. Perhaps I had loved him as if he, only he, were the half of me that gave completeness to my human existence.

I had lost my other half, was a wretched fragment from then on, for all time.

Slowly, very slowly, we learned a little bit more every day about the situation in which we found ourselves after the battle, so that we could adjust ourselves to the reality of our changed lives.

Of my four brothers, only one had survived the battle on Mount Gilboa, Ishbosheth, who was the least close to me, much older than I, I scarcely knew him and do not recall ever having had a conversation with him.

I did not even like to look at him, that short, fat man with his puffy eyes that started indolently. He moved to Mahanaim, a city on the east bank of the Jordan. Oh, what, he did not move. He was ordered there by Saul's Commander-in-Chief, Abner, who had also survived the battle.

One day the thickset, bull-necked man stood in our house, too, and said in a hard, imperious tone: "You will have to settle in Mahanaim as well. I want all the children of my king who are still living to be together." At first I did not understand why he wanted that, but soon I began to comprehend that he wanted to build up a counterforce against David in Mahanaim.

At that time, David was already King of Judah, his own tribe in Hebron.

I was to serve as a tool for Abner to use against David. If it had not been so sad, I would have laughed out loud.

But I was surprised that Palti dared to contradict him: "I want to stay with my animals."

Abner had taken no notice of Palti up to this moment, now he looked at him in astonishment and said cursorily: "You will get new ones. Also new fields if you wish."

Palti wanted neither new animals nor new fields, but Abner, who was a soldier, not a farmer, could not comprehend that.

After this almost quiet protest, Palti said nothing more.

Abner knew his strength. There was nothing left for us but to obey.

Why, really? Who was he, Abner, a general without an army, a loyal vassal without a king, a commander who had lost a great battle and survived by chance?

Why did we not say no in Gibeah? We were too young, too inexperienced to know that saying no is always, or at least almost always, a possibility and often the better one. What could Abner have done to us? Killed us? And if he did? Neither one of us put all that much value on our lives. Besides, he would have refrained from doing harm to me, a daughter of Saul.

We had both been taught to do what we were told. Obedience, something that went without saying.

It was a dark hour when we submitted to Abner.

Thus had association with me brought misfortune to Palti just as it had to David.

I wept a little, Palti put his arm around my shoulder and dried my tears with a cloth.

It took three days until we had made all of our preparations and could leave, with the small escort that Abner had sent us for protection. Across the Jordan, into the mountainous country, to Mahanaim, that foreign, threatening city.

Palti and I did not live as peacefully in Mahanaim as we would have wished, war was everywhere. Abner, no less ambitious than David, even if with less luck and radiance, waged war against the Philistines and many other peoples, in the end, however, against his own people, against all tribes that still stood by David. Here Benjamin, in other words Saul, there Judah, hence David, was the rallying cry.

This war between brothers was deplorable and was waged harder by both sides than against an enemy from without. Palti was no soldier, and did not need to be one, could still till the fields that had recently been given to him, and I was permitted to remain at home without interference. Patiently waiting for whatever would come. That I was used to since I was little, not a new, not an unusual situation.

Men on opposite sides killing each other and creating fear for the women. Thus Jahwe wills it and all find it quite natural. I cannot imagine a God who wishes and permits that. I cannot imagine our invisible, omnipotent, omnipresent God at all. Would it not be enough to believe in him? Oh, but I could never just believe and cannot even now on the threshold of death.

Many times Palti came home complaining: soldiers, our own or foreign ones, had trampled his fields to pieces and all his work had been in vain.

I comforted him as well as I could.

Besides that, everything in Mahanaim remained foreign to us.

Since Jonathan's death I no longer heard much of David, learned only as much as anyone else.

That he had a new wife again, Maacha, the daughter of the King of Geshur, whose tiny kingdom bordered on Mahanaim, in other words, was strategically very favorably located in the event it came to open warfare between David and Ishbosheth.

Maacha, she, too, young and beautiful, had borne David two children, a son Absalom, and a daughter Tamar.

The women told each other the news at the well. And although I seldom went there, even here I was indeed the sister of the king, the rumors eventually reached me.

The women said that Abner was openly arming against David and would soon cross the Jordan with his troops.

But they were also of the opinion that he would prefer to negotiate with David because he considered him to have a more promising future than Ishbosheth. I think they knew everything exactly, even before it occurred.

Yet another rumor: Ishbosheth and Abner were no longer on good terms because Abner was living with Rizpah, who had been Saul's concubine and had had children by him. Everyone knows that whoever sleeps with the concubine of a king is also laying claim to the throne. That displeased Ishbosheth, who overestimated his power and was laughably proud of being king. That he was so only by Abner's grace he seemed to have forgotten.

And again comes a day when Abner visits us, that bearer of ill fortune with the bull neck and hard mouth. It is not a visit out of politeness, that well I know him. Serious and unfriendly he says: "Listen, Michal, I have begun negotiations with David. That is better than waging war against a man who is stronger when all is said and done. I want what is best for the people of Israel just as he does. It is possible that the tribes will unite under him. He is in agreement with my plans, and why not? But he has made one stipulation: that you come back to him."

Forceful pounding of the heart, this is the moment for which I have lived for years, which I have longed for in my innermost being. I can return to him, yes, he demands it. Not out of love, I make no pretense to myself about that. If he loved me, he would long since have found some possibility of coming to me.

My gaze falls upon Palti, who again has been overlooked by Abner as if he were not in the room. He is pale, his lips tremble, his big nose twitches up and down. "What does Ishbosheth have to say about that?" I ask, just to say something. "He is agreed, does not find the demand improper, you are certainly David's lawfully betrothed first wife. Tomorrow we set out, I will accompany you, you will receive from me a she-ass upon which you will ride. The way to Hebron is long." "Why so hasty?" I ask without getting an answer.

I think back on the night, the last in which Palti and I lie beside each other and touch one another exactly as little as in the many preceding nights.

The pain of separation tears me apart from top to bottom. Do I still love David? No longer? If I only knew what that is: love. Then, yes, when I was an inexperienced maiden in my father's palace, when I thought unceasingly of him, David, full of longing, rapture, then I thought I knew.

Now this good man Palti is lying beside me weeping and cannot comprehend that I will leave him. Want to leave him? Oh, Jahwe, I do not know. "Do not go," he says, "stay. Who would do anything to you if you refuse?"

I contradict him with better reasons than in Gibeah. "You do not know David. He will not do anything to me, that is true. But he will not put up with being refused something that belongs to him. He will take me away from here by force and that means war. I would be guilty of the death of everyone who fell in that battle. That I cannot take upon myself. Do you understand?" Palti nods. With him I can talk, something I could never do with David. And because he sees that there is no way out of our situation, he falls silent.

In the morning I go to Ishbosheth, small, twisted, and fat, sitting upon his throne, which is adorned with colorfully painted wood carvings. He winks at me with his puffy eyes: "Are you content, Michal?" I shake my head, not ready to say anything about myself to this brother who is so distant, so foreign to me. "Oh no, not content? But once upon a time you wanted to marry this David at any price." "The price was too high," I say without expression.

"You mean the foreskins of the Philistines." He laughs as if it were a good joke. "Do not be sentimental, sister, that is an old story."

Yes, it is an old story, but it has determined my life.

It is a hot day. I ride, Palti runs along behind, holds on to the tail of the she-ass. If it were not summer, we would not be able to get across the Jordan. Now the fords are easily passable, the water reaches only to the fetlocks of my she-ass.

I turn around toward Palti. I do not want to think about it, that he will soon be gone, gone forever. He is alive and yet, for me, it is as if he were dead. My protector. From now on I no longer have a protector. Palti, whom I like as if he were a brother. And again the uncertainty of what love is.

We have the Jordan behind us, the way to Hebron is clear. Abner, who has not let himself be seen till now, comes galloping up on his black stallion and says to Palti in a commanding tone: "You will turn back now. I cannot use you here."

Palti embraces me. For the last time I sense the familiar, dry smell, mixed with a faint odor of goat stall. "Do not go," I say, but know that he will go. Abner is standing behind us with his sword. Oh, if we had the courage to say no, the courage to resist. We do not have it. Are cowardly in a moment that called for bravery.

Palti quickly slips me a dagger, tells me that I may need it. I mount, turn around once more, see him standing there, small, ugly, and already very far away.

Abner rides along beside me and says from the height of his saddle: "Daughter of my king, I am taking you toward a great goal. You will have influence upon David. Make a good king out of him, he shall unite the tribes of Israel and found a great empire. A wise woman once prophesied to me: one day a light will go forth from Bethlehem, that will illuminate the world."

You overestimate my influence, I would like to say, do not say it, because I would then have to explain to him that I do not want to have any influence, I want to live, nothing more. But this man will never understand that.

No longer be a tool of politics. Ride over a land in which there is no longer war.

Live one's own life. Peace, the single important goal, the precondition for everything else.

~~ _T_ H E L O N G winter is past, the long, hard, winter in Yerushalayim. It has snowed a little and the sky above the white sandstone of the houses is of a deep, dark blue.

I, Michal, have been quite unwell during these months and actually still am. I did not have a sickness that one could call by a name unless one were to admit that old age, in and of itself, is a sickness.

I no longer have much appetite, not for eating, nor for living, am tired from morning till evening, when I arise early in the morning I would just as soon lie down again immediately, am tired, unhappy, empty, so empty that there is not even any pain left in me over those who are dead. A little something flares up: longing for the lost pain. Why do I get up in the morning at all? I do not want to set a bad example for my young servants, fill them with a barren fear of growing old. Do not want them to say: now she does not even have enough strength left to stay on her feet, yet not so very long ago, she was the first one up in the morning and was happy. It is sad, sad is the life that goes by so fast and ends so miserably.

So I pull myself together, remain silent, still try to give a good appearance. How should the young face up to life when we old ones show them that everything is in vain.

I have found out that they have already noticed my sorrow by the tone of my voice and so I want to go on telling my story quietly to myself and will continue where I stopped, at the journey from Mahanaim to Hebron to see David again.

So be it.

My she-ass is limping when we finally arrive in Hebron, the distance we have covered was great.

In the evening after Palti has turned back at Abner's command, the soldiers erect a tent for me alone. I do not need to sleep on the ground, they have put together for me a soft bed of pelts that sways when I climb up on it. There I lie and listen to the wind, hear the slatting noise when it gets into the stretched fabric flaps of the tent and blows them up and down.

When I walk out of the tent in the morning, the desert is glowing red and yellow in the first beams of the sun. I breathe in the still-fresh air. And then, slowly and majestically, across a steep ravine comes a large, light-colored animal with gigantic, almost artistically turned horns that run out to striking, backward curves at the ends, an ibex, that looks at me almost reverently, with large, moist, brown eyes.

My heart pounds violently, suddenly the feeling: this animal is David or at least someone sent by him, so incomparably proud, so noble. I take a step toward it.

It stands there, motionless, but when two soldiers with

spears suddenly appear back behind the tent and I throw up my arms in horror, the animal at first takes a few startled steps on the spot and then walks away slowly and full of dignity.

When we have crossed the Jordan and ride through a broad valley with gentle hills, past gigantic herds of sheep with long, brown fleeces, the landscape becomes familiar to me. At home in Gibeah it looked quite similar: green hills strewn with stones and large herds.

Outside Hebron, Abner is at my side again.

He sits high above me on his horse, the sign of his rank, this thickset one whom I do not like, who is too much man for me.

He has told me much in these days, of things and events that interested me. An introduction to David's life as King of Judah. But I had no way of telling when he was correct and when he was mistaken. I did not even know how honest his intentions were. With David. With me.

He told about the other wives, of Abigail whom he called a splendid woman and of Maacha whom he named a wild Arab girl.

He told of David's shrewd adviser, Ahithophel of Gilo, whom he termed the cleverest Jew and consequently the cleverest man among all peoples, because it is indeed well known that the Jews are shrewder than all others.

He did not say, perhaps did not even know, that this Ahithophel had a son by the name of Eliam and he a daughter: Bathsheba. Who mentions people so unimportant to the story? That Bathsheba was not so unimportant, neither of us knew then. As yet, there was no such person present at David's court.

Our fortune, our misfortune: to know nothing. My father had banished all soothsayers from our country and I believe that he did right. Perhaps I would have turned around on the spot, had I had any premonition of the trouble that lay before us. The way things were, I could still expect everything and hope for everything.

What was I expecting?

Did I really believe that things would go on from where they had stopped or even earlier, when David was my beloved? No, I did not believe that. Pessimistic by nature, I am more inclined to believe that everything just gets worse, and life has mostly proved me right.

While we rode, Abner also reported about David's three nephews, sons of his sister Zeruiah, who had been with him from the beginning and had borne all of the burdens of the fugitive's life with him. David had made Joab, the eldest, his Commander-in-Chief. Abner did not like him, no wonder, both were commanders, each one begrudged the other a victorious battle. Later, Joab became Abner's murderer, but, as already said, none of that had happened yet.

Abner became silent, he had spoken of three sons of Zeruiah, but for the moment he did not tell anything about the third one.

When he did later, his voice sounded distressed: "Zeruiah's third son was called Asahel. He was young, handsome, and slender, a joy to behold, the fastest runner among David's followers, loved by all, especially by David, who doted on him.

"Joab and I had arranged a meeting on the shore of the little lake at Gibeon.

"We wanted to discuss important things, the uniting of the northern and southern kingdoms under David's sovereignty, because we were both striving for that, he as well as I.

"Each one of us had the same number of armed men with him, among which were Joab's brothers.

"We arranged war games, but everything was to proceed strictly according to the rules, everything was agreed upon, the number of paces that could be taken, the distances from one another. The field was marked out; the three sons of Zeruiah and I took our places on a podium that had been quickly put together and which made it possible for us to observe the events from above.

"In the beginning it looked like a magnificent, artfully rehearsed dance, but then it happened suddenly: no one kept to the rules anymore. The men hacked at each other with their swords, dead and wounded were carried from the melee. The ground was red with blood. My men were defeated, had to give way, I followed along behind my men during the ignominious retreat. Suddenly I noticed that a man was pursuing me. I recognized Asahel who was running after me, swinging his sword. He had removed his breastplate in order to run faster.

" 'Stop,' I shouted, 'I mean you no harm, but if you come too close to me I will have to kill you.' He did not listen to me, did not stop chasing me, and when he was quite close to me, he threatened me with his sword. Then I, who am much more experienced in battle, turned to face him and struck him in the body with the butt-end of my spear. Perhaps I had hoped in this way I would not kill him, one really does not know what one thinks at such a moment. Be that as it may, he fell over and did not move again. I did not want to do it, Michal, especially because of David, whom I did not want to offend for the sake of the alliance.

"Why Asahel was pursuing me, a beaten opponent who, indeed, was almost an ally, I did not understand and still do not understand. But there are men, Michal, who go into a frenzy when they see blood.

"Since then I fear Asahel's brothers and their revenge. It would not help me at all if I said that it was he who attacked me and not I him. They would not believe me. The dead are always right, Michal. I did not kill him willingly, but I had no other choice."

It was the first time that a person told me that he had killed another human being. I shuddered. But I remained silent.

As we approached Hebron, Abner came to talk about David's carefully thought-out administration, which differed greatly from that of King Saul.

Despite the small size of Judah, David had set up an entire series of ministries and filled them all with capable men. There were also many and influential musicians whom David addressed as if they were his brothers. He was indeed one of them and quite certainly the best.

Abner told further of Maacha's two children, of David's favorite Absalom and the charming, little Tamar, he also spoke of David's firstborn, Amnon, the son of the Jezreelite Ahinoam who had already died. Abner did not think much of Amnon. Thought he was unbridled and inconsiderate.

We now ride down one of the low hills, then up to Hebron and turn into the courtyard of David's palace. From the courtyard a large open stairway leads upward along the wall of squared stones. On the lowest steps stand two amphoras filled with pink blossoms, between them someone moves.

A rather graceful, blond, bearded man. Can it be he? In our land there are not many blond people.

My knees buckle as I climb from the she-ass. The blond man has walked over to me and catches me in his arms as I stagger.

It is he, it is. I sense him, smell him. His beard tickles me strangely.

I do not know whether I should laugh or weep at this moment, for which I have lived so many years.

"It has taken a long time," says David, says it with his beautiful, clear voice, which I immediately recognize, "much longer than I wished. But Jahwe willed it so. We must submit to his will. It is astonishing how little the years have done to you. You are still beautiful, my little Michal."

The words sound as if all could still be well between us, but I know that nothing would go well any longer. Too much that has passed stands between us, is not to be obliterated. Not the foreskins of the Philistines, not Saul's glaring hatred, not Jonathan's quiet love.

At the thought of my brother tears run down my face. David wipes them away with a soft cloth and says, as if he has guessed my thoughts: "Do not cry, Michal. Jonathan has gone on ahead of us and will always be with us."

Words, I think, beautiful words without meaning. The dead are not always with us.

David leads me up the stairs into his throne room, which is undecorated and pleases me. The throne is a huge, unadorned chair.

David puts his arm around me, leads me to the throne and forces me, with gentle pressure of his arm, to sit there. I make myself quite small and think amusedly that if someone came in, he would not see me, would not know that there was a woman upon this throne. David stands before me laughing. Mischief sparkles in his eyes, suddenly he is the shepherd from Bethlehem again, a boy who has gotten away with some exuberant trick. "We do not know what it is to have a queen," he says, "that is a shame, I would like to see you crowned, my queen, the coronet would look good on your dark hair."

He lets himself down on one knee before me, takes my hand, and kisses it.

I play along, am moved as I do it, say: "Arise, my king, I thank you." I am moved because I see how little the difficult time as a fugitive has changed him.

"Sing me a song, my king," I ask and he must hear from my voice how very much I wish that.

He stands up, calls a servant and has the harp brought to him.

Now I am sitting on the throne like Saul, David stands a little distance away from me and sings:

> Blessed is the man
> Who has not walked in the council of the wicked,
> Nor tread the way of sin,
> Nor sat in the seat of scoffers,
> But has his delight in the law of the Lord
> And meditates on His law day and night;
> He will be
> Like a tree planted by a watercourse,
> That yields its fruit in its season
> And its leaf does not wither:
> In all that he does, he succeeds.
> Not so are the wicked,
> But like unto chaff that the wind scatters.
> Therefore the wicked will not withstand judgment,
> Nor sinners stand in the congregation of the righteous,
> For He knows the way of the righteous, but the way of the
>   wicked will perish.

His voice trails off quite softly in sadness. And there it is again, the happiness, the rapture, the soaring above the earth.

His voice is more masculine, but it has become even more beautiful, rejoicing, sad, and proud of the presence of God, of being the Chosen One.

I have put my head in my hands, tears run between my fingers. But I see that David, too, the tree by the watercourse, the righteous one, has moist eyes, the singing has exalted him as it does each and every time, has made him happy. Carefully he puts the harp down. Comes to me, takes me in his arms, we are moved and belong together as once long ago in our first night of love.

Gently David parts from me, claps his hands. Through the curtain of strings of blue and green beads that separates off the room, comes a beautiful, no longer entirely young woman with a regal bearing, who wears her dark blond hair braided and wound around her head. "This is Abigail," says David. She stretches both hands toward me: "Welcome, Michal. I am happy that you are here." So matter-of-fact, so warm. She points to the harp and says: "You have gotten our king to play the harp. And surely he sang at the same time. That he does very rarely nowadays." We embrace and kiss each other and are devoted to one another from this hour on.

It is one of the great moments in the history of the world, history holds its breath, when it turns out that two women who love the same man, also like each other. Woe betide them if they do not realize that and let the great hour slip away unused, fritter their time away in quarrels and petty jealousy and woe to the man whom they claim to love, whom, however, they will drag into misery along with them, because each of them views him as her possession and is busily occupied with doing harm to this possession and herself as well.

David belonged neither to me nor to her, we both understood that, my beautiful Abigail and I, we made life easier for him and have both been contented.

How different it was when Bathsheba came, with her demands that could never be satisfied and her rejection of everyone who would not lie admiringly at her feet.

Twice David claps his hands, again the bead curtain parts, in comes a slender, shy creature, a nomad, who would fit better in a tent than in a palace. Clad in a simple, gray garment, girdled only around the middle with gold. Her arms are around two children. As soon as she turns her head, the pieces of her gold and turquoise earrings strike each other and give off a melodious ring.

I know that it is Maacha, the daughter of the King of Geshur, but she could just as well be a shepherdess. She is beautiful. Her children are beautiful. The boy, dark like his mother, with thick tousled hair, yet he has David's beaming, slanted, gray eyes. Incredible contrast. Breathtaking. Absalom: Jahwe must take satisfaction in him, if human beauty means anything to him.

The girl resembles her mother, is very dark, with melancholy, deep, black eyes that seem to anticipate every sorrow.

David calls the boy to him: "This is Absalom, not only my favorite, but Jahwe's as well."

Yes, he knows it exactly, but I am uneasy at these words which are intended to conjure up a kind fate, but will perhaps call down Jahwe's wrath.

I take leave of Maacha and the children, Abigail leads me to my rooms, which she has furnished with great care. Everything she touches becomes beauty and splendor in her hands.

We talk to one another for a long time and I notice her anxiety over David's doting on Absalom. I know that Abigail and David's only son, Chileab, died as a small child. In our land, children die more often than they remain alive. One cannot do anything about that.

Even on this first day I meet up with David's Highest Priest Abiathar. No longer the crying, distraught boy in my house back then, a proud, hard, and perhaps even vain man. He looks at me coolly, nods weakly in my direction, and does not show the slightest sign that he has ever seen me before.

Such an icy coldness issues forth from him that I ask myself: can such a man be a priest? He is no comforter of men, that I see immediately, no intermediary between them and Jahwe, sternly he serves his stern God.

David introduces me to his prophet Nathan as well. He does not give the impression of being a prophet or at least as I, probably recalling Samuel, imagined a prophet to be. Nathan is very tall, with a well-formed head from which dark, lively, and very intelligent eyes scrutinize me. He could be a poet, and later, judging by the parables that he composed, it turned out that he was a poet.

I live very quietly and withdrawn in the time that follows, see David rarely. He usually comes unannounced and only when he has something to discuss that has to do with his kingdom. He must think that as the daughter of a king I have to be interested in the affairs of state. I do not detract from this belief and listen attentively to his stories.

He never makes an attempt to sleep with me. Perhaps I wish he would, in any case I would not refuse any longer, all that lies far behind. But I am also not the one who can begin it, so we live on beside each other as brother and sister or like

Michal and Palti, whose sacrifice of abstinence has lost its meaning now.

Palti is dead. I have not been in Hebron long when a man from Mahanaim brings the news. He was not sick long, had a fever that felled him after just one night.

Perhaps he cried out for me in his last hours. Perhaps he passed over without thinking anything else of me than that I deserted him, the most loyal of men, for a phantom called David.

"Did he ask for me?" I ask. "I do not know," says the messenger.

"Who sent you?"

"The king."

I know nothing, learn nothing, and believe that it is better not to know. But it is a guilt that I will bear my whole life long: that I did not find the courage to say no a single time: No, I will not go, I will not leave Palti.

When I scream, weep, and rave, Abigail takes me in her arms and says imploringly: "Dear one, you must adjust to it."

And how does one do that? How does one adjust? And if I do not, if I do not want to adjust to it?

Then I would have to kill myself, but I am not ready for that, am still too curious about what will come.

Now, in old age, curiosity is past, I can adjust more easily. Even now it is still difficult. But the dead persuade. Out of the graves grow flowers, trees. And I think: just as the decaying body is transformed and something new arises from it, so must it be with the soul.

There will no longer be the soul of Michal, the strong soul of Jonathan, the good soul of Palti. Like the decomposing flesh, the soul will disintegrate into infinitely many pieces and something new will sprout forth, perhaps something never thought of, never felt until now.

In that I believe more than in Jahwe.

One day David comes to me, storms in furiously, contrary to his usual fashion. He is angry, strikes the wall with his clenched right hand.

"What is it, David?"

I see that he is trembling, he paces back and forth in agitation, and says with a strained, foreign voice: "Joab, that butcher, has killed Abner."

Thus was the word spoken that for me would never again be separated from the person of Joab.

"Abner was my guest, we parted in peace. Joab caused him to turn back under some pretense and murdered him. Here, in Hebron, he will be buried with a funeral that is worthy of one of the great men of Israel. Joab has gotten Abner out of the way, not just out of blood-revenge for Asahel, but because he did not want Abner to share in making me king over all Israel. For that I should be indebted to him alone and now I must prove that I am not guilty of the death of this great man."

He is beside himself, I have never seen him this way before. Everything that he says makes sense. But I now think that his anger was also so great because Abner would have played an important role in the unification of Israel and perhaps could not be replaced by anyone else.

The funeral ceremonies last three days. David, who has fasted the whole day, walks behind the bier and, in a voice choked with tears, delivers his elegy for Abner to the entire populace and to Joab:

Rend your garments,
Gird on sackcloth
And lament for Abner!
Should an Abner die like one despised?
May God do so to me, yea even more,
If I taste bread or anything else before the setting of the sun.
Do you not realize that a supreme and great man fell this day
    in Israel?
But I am weak this day, though anointed king,
Too hard are these men for me, the sons of Zeruiah.
May the Lord repay the evildoer according to his wickedness!

He had censured Joab publicly, but he still needed him, without Joab no conquest of Yerushalayim, without Joab no dead Uriah.

He was tied to this man. What did Joab know about him? I often wondered why he did not free himself from the butcher and could never, never even till David's death, entirely solve this puzzle.

When David was already a dying man, he charged his successor Solomon, the most unloved of his children, not to allow Joab to die in peace, which he carried out immediately and had Joab executed, no reconciliation, no mildness, hatred right to the grave. Yes, thus was he, was David, my beloved, my husband.

It is not long until the news of another death comes, and again from Mahanaim.

Ishbosheth, the incompetent king installed by Abner, had been beheaded by two of his officers while he slept.

The murderers themselves come, probably hoping for a reward, and bring as proof of their deed Ishbosheth's head, carefully wrapped in a cloth, and lay it down before David, who does not tolerate murderers of a king in his presence and has the two of them executed immediately.

I was not very sad about the death of Ishbosheth even though I would have wished a more peaceful end for this unloved brother.

I was sad because David had the two murderers executed. That my artist-king should not have done. For me he was the poet, singer, musician for whom it was not fitting to be Lord over life and death.

The plans for the unification of all Israel had become more realistic through the death of Ishbosheth. The northern kingdom no longer had a ruler. There remained only one king now: David.

The elders of all the tribes came to Hebron, they elected David king and anointed him.

He was thirty years old, a man in the fullness of vigor, who had nearly completed half of his life and knew it as well.

There were all sorts of ceremonies and festivities. Naturally, we women remained at home and had the servants tell us about the anointing and coronation of David.

At his next visit, just as on my first day in Hebron, he kneels down on one knee, this game seems to please him.

"How much I would like to have you at my side during our celebrations, you are the daughter of a king and would make a good appearance as queen. But the women have to remain silent in the council of men. That is the law of the world which prescribes that the men shall do the deeds and the women shall serve the men."

Forever and ever, amen, I think, do not say it because I have the hope, no, even more, the conviction that the day will come, the beautiful, bright day, when women will be admitted to the council to restrain the men from all too rash actions for which they can no longer make amends, from playing with weapons, with danger.

The day when women will no longer be merchandise in the markets, when everyone, men and women, will harken to the song of life, and understand.

A little later, David appears in my quarters again, more agitated than usual, however not angrily as after Abner's death, I see that he is moved by great joy.

He lets himself down on my bed, beckons me to sit beside him, takes my hand, holds it tightly, then he speaks: "Now that by the will of Jahwe I am king over all Israel—the road was long, my little Michal, from the shepherd in Bethlehem to the leader of our people—now Hebron is no longer a suitable capital, too small, too easily conquered, situated too far to the south. And Mahanaim, on the other side of the Jordan, too far to the north.

"Perhaps Gibeah," I suggest, although I know that he does not expect any opinion from me at all.

He shakes his head vigorously: "Gibeah, no, that lies in the middle of the realm of the Benjamites, that was good for Saul, is nothing for me, one from Judah. But there is, situated nearly exactly in the center of the country and, best of all, belonging to no tribe, the high, almost uncapturable rock fortress Zion. Of course the Jebusites, who are hostile to us, live there, but on what their claim to it is based is not known to me. It can be taken from them; even if it will not be easy—they boast that their city could even be defended by the blind and the lame. Yerushalayim, the City of David, it will be called, for now and all time."

He has spoken passionately, he has become flushed as if he had a fever. He stands up, steps back a few paces, stretches out his right hand, closes his eyes: "Do you not see it, the pale-yellow city, sparkling in the glow of the setting sun? My city, from which no one will ever cast me out, the City of David, my personal property, which will bear my name and my glory on to distant times."

A vision, the vision of a poet, but also that of a conqueror, for whom there is no obstacle. He sees it before him, his possession, his legacy to Israel, to his people.

And the dream became reality. He conquered the fortress with cunning. They told of a spring that gave rise to a small stream, in whose bed David and his men, Joab in the lead, had clambered up to overwhelm the unsuspecting Jebusites.

And again Joab, Joab the butcher, to whom he owed thanks anew.

꧁ *A* C O O L summer morning be-
fore a scorching hot day. I, old Michal, have had Sulamith, my
maidservant, accompany me into the garden quite early, even
before the gray dawn gave way to the brightness of the morning, so as to have something of the fresh air.

Beneath the great olive tree Sulamith has lovingly prepared
a bed of blankets and pillows for me, on which I can stretch
out completely. Sitting too long tires me, my legs swell up, but
this way I can lie quite relaxed and feel well. How long have I
been living here, in Yerushalayim, in the City of David? Many,
many years, I have not counted them, counting years is not a
custom with us, we let them slip by as if they were a string of
pearls. For me, it is as if I had never lived elsewhere.

After our people had conquered the city, we moved from
Hebron to the southern side of the hill called Ophel, from
which one can see, far in the distance, the low hills which

stretch out over the land until just in front of the sea. Quite close by, on the left, is the beautiful height covered with old olive trees called the Mount of Olives because of the trees, above which the morning sun rises.

I liked Yerushalayim immediately, better than Hebron with its smallness. Abigail and I lived in two houses that stood next to each other, did almost everything in common, passed our days together. Abigail, my unexpected, my late joy.

David very soon had a palace built for himself of yellowish-white sandstone and cedarwood from Lebanon, a beautiful structure, even if much plainer than the palace in which I now live. Solomon is a lordly builder, for whom nothing can be luxurious enough, nothing splendid enough, he indulges his rich, often extravagant imagination in his buildings, in the palace, and, above all, in the temple which he has had erected for Jahwe and the Ark of the Covenant.

We had not yet been living in Yerushalayim very long when the thing happened that set me and David far apart.

In the early days, he often roamed around outside the city. I must get to know the surroundings, he said. How shall I defend my city if I do not know every rampart and every height?

During his visits, which were becoming more and more infrequent, he often told me of a place where he especially liked to stop, a shady grove of balsam trees and bushes, and of a remarkable phenomenon that he had noticed there. "When the evening wind comes, and it starts up every day not long before sunset, there is a sound in the treetops as if marching soldiers are approaching. You must come out there with me sometime, to hear it yourself." It never came to the point that he took me out with him, either he had forgotten it or the event that separated us had already occurred. I do not even know whether I would have perceived that which he heard with his sensitive musician's ears. Certainly the soldiers heard it later as well, so it surely must have been more than imagination.

When the Philistines learned that David had become king over all Israel, they gathered together once again to destroy him.

Since he had become a vassal of their long-dead King Achish, David was not on bad terms with them. He grasped, as always and everywhere, each opportunity to learn something. From them he had learned how to forge weapons and build ships. That they could do very well, since they had once come from far across the sea, from a distant island called Crete. The Jews were not a seafaring people, they had no wish to put themselves at the mercy of a foreign, often dangerous, and never controllable element. So much did David trust the Philistines that he later assembled his bodyguard from them. They were called, half in jest, half admiringly, the Cherethites and Pelethites, after their homeland and their race.

Now, however, they wanted to conquer David, who had become king of their archenemies, the Jews, and had drawn up in the valley of Rephaim south of the city.

And again we feared an approaching enemy, but in this battle David defeated the Philistines once and for all. They never again made an attempt to fall upon us. After this decisive victory, David was also able to bring back home the ark of the covenant, which had been kept for a long time by the Philistines.

Before the battle David had ordered his men into the grove of balsam trees. The far more numerous enemies considered themselves just so much more secure, the longer the day went on. Because David had not drawn up in front of them with his men, the Philistines said to themselves, it will soon be dark, David will not attack so late. He had told his soldiers, however, they should wait in the grove until they heard the noise of the marching men in the treetops, and only then were they to make a flanking movement far to the right and attack the Philistines in the rear.

Later he said the command for the unusual order of battle had issued from Jahwe himself.

He stands before his palace, his blond hair falling over his face, he looks a little tired and very happy.

Surely he comprehends immediately the finality of this victory and has the proud feeling of having freed Israel from its enemy for all time.

He brought back the ark of the covenant from the Philistines and thereby happened the thing that estranged us.

At first he was ill-humored because he was not permitted to house the ark in a temple, but only in a tent.

And when David was in an ill humor, the earth trembled.

Nathan, his prophet, had told him that it would not be pleasing to Jahwe if David built a temple to him, he had spilled too much blood already. Only his son and successor would be permitted to undertake the building of the temple.

Besides, Jahwe had become accustomed to living in a tent and could continue to do so.

Why did he say that? Why did David obey him? Naturally Nathan wanted to obtain more and more influence over the king and David obeyed him because his conscience was no longer so clean, even before the affair with Uriah.

Therefore no temple, just a tent. Despite that, the ark was to be brought into the city with great pomp on a cart drawn by oxen.

At the head of a great procession with all the musicians who lived at the court, David hurried out to bring home the ark from the house of Abinadab on the hill.

The two sons of Abinadab, Uzzah and Ahio, walked along beside the cart. Uzzah, a young priest, very excited over the honor of being allowed to accompany the ark.

At a narrow spot in the bumpy road, the oxen stumbled and the ark started to slide from the cart.

Then Uzzah reached out and grasped the ark with his hand in order to hold it back. The excitement was too much for the young priest and he fell over dead on the spot.

David was frightened. Was Uzzah's death the result of Jahwe's anger because Uzzah had touched the ark? Abiathar and Nathan supported this interpretation: it will bring misfortune if the ark is touched.

But one can only touch something that is there. Thus David resolved not to bring the ark into Yerushalayim. He commanded the cart drivers to turn off to the house of Obededom the Gittite.

There the ark remained for three months. David inquired anxiously now and then whether all was in order in the house of Obed. Not only was everything in good order, but he learned that Obed was, at this time, clearly blessed. Then David resolved to bring the ark to Yerushalayim, to the tent that stood ready for it there. The ark, a rectangular, gilded case of locust wood, with a cover on which stood two gilt cherubs, was our most sacred object. Many believed that Jahwe lived in it, something that I could never quite understand. Why should our omnipresent God have settled into such a small box?

The ark's second return home to Yerushalayim was to be marked by even greater ceremony. David had practiced with his musicians for days on end. When I looked out through the window of my house, I was astonished that he was dressed like an ordinary priest, in nothing more than a linen loincloth. This time they had had the oxen that pulled the cart walk over the same stretch several times. They knew the way and it was unlikely that they would stumble again. Every inhabitant, even every woman, was to receive a loaf of bread, a cluster of dates, and a raisin cake.

With loud fanfare and blaring trumpets the ark drew into the city. Everything had been exactly preordained and directed by David. First of all a steer and a fatted calf were slaughtered as a sacrifice to Jahwe, then came the procession. David had organized choruses of boys, their clear voices sounded happy. They sang their songs alternately, once from close by, then from a distance.

I was not sad that nobody had invited me to be there; I did not like crowds at all. (Abigail, however, who loved celebrations, had immediately gone out into the street.) But I was still curious enough to take a place at the window so as not to miss anything. The colorful show looked especially beautiful from above. Suddenly, without my knowing why and how he had entered, Abiathar was standing beside me.

David was now dancing on in front of the ox-cart. He was really no longer a youth, but a stately man. Yet he whirled in circles, hopped and sprang so that his short loincloth flew up and the maidservants giggled and pointed their fingers at him. Then I was seized by anger over this shameless display and when my anger had subsided, I had to laugh. Perhaps just because I had become so angry. I laughed and pressed my kerchief to my face so that my laughter could not be heard, but Abiathar noticed it.

He looked at me indignantly. I thought, now he will strike me. But he did not permit himself to go so far. But later, when David came in for a moment, Abiathar pointed his finger at me: "She laughed, during a holy ceremony she laughed at the king. May she be cursed, she shall be barren forever."

David looked at me. He knew that the curse would be fulfilled: a woman who has not been together with any man is unlikely to have children. Then David's face broke into laughter; he slapped his naked thighs and grunted: "Never a child. She is a barren woman, who is worthless."

The laughter had gone out of me. I could sense how something had shattered between David and me.

In the evening I lie on my bed and weep. Weep for David, for myself, for my love, for my squandered youth. The noise of the festivities still forces its way through the grillwork over the window. This day, on which David was exalted and I humiliated, is a turning point.

꧁ *How* long have I, old Grete, been living in Germany, the land of my murderers, the land of my language? I have never regretted coming back to the place I came from and have never wanted to be anywhere else.

In the autumn of 1947 I returned for the first time.

Two Dutch boys led me and a friend through woods and heath for four hours one night, took us over the "green border" because the Allies had absolutely no intention of permitting anyone with the passport of a displaced person to enter the country. It was a beautiful night and I was quite drunk with the joy of being outside again, of breathing in the smell of rotting leaves, of having the soft, springy earth under my feet.

We carried no money, cigarettes were our only currency, because we knew that the English locked up any foreigner they caught for a longer time if he had money with him. Six weeks in jail were to be expected in the worst case. What did that mean when you had been in danger of your life, hunted, pursued for four years? Six weeks in an English prison? Why not? But it never came to that. Nobody noticed us.

At the window of a tiny railroad station, we asked for two tickets to Neuss (Could you really do that? You could.) and pushed two cigarettes toward the ticket agent.

My friend wanted to visit her sister who had survived in Germany as the wife in a mixed marriage. I wanted to see an old friend, Urs, whom I had seen for the last time after Waiki's death in 1941. At that time we had decided to stay together after the war. That I, a Jewish woman in occupied Holland and he, a young German facing military service, would both survive was quite out of the question. A miracle in which we frivolously believed and which came true.

I had found out that he was alive and working as a director at the theater in Darmstadt but I did not know whether I would still be willing to live with him after four such years. I wanted to find out, so I was in a hurry to get to Germany.

The train to Neuss, like all trains in those days, was overcrowded, my friend got a seat, I stood in the corridor because I did not want to give up one moment of the joy of hearing all the people around me speaking German. A warm bath in the language I still loved, in which I thought, dreamed, and hoped to write.

Beside me stood a gaunt man (all men were gaunt) with an intelligent face. He stared at me a long time, then said: "You remind me of Rosa Luxemburg." At first I found that hardly flattering, but then I grasped what an incredible compliment he was paying me. He said: "You're coming from abroad and are a Jew." I nodded (now, finally, I could admit to it). He said softly: "How beautiful. I live in Solingen and have just started a social unity party there. Come with me. Stay with me." I shook my head: "I'm not alone." "Too bad. Think it over anyway."

In all the years in Holland, no man had ever invited me to come with him. It was different here. Different air. Great familiarity.

In Frankfurt, a city in which I had lived for a long time before the war, we walked from the main railroad station toward Sachsenhausen, where my friend's sister lived. First walk through a city in ruins. "Impossible to live here," said my friend. But I thought: we'll see.

On the way back from Sachsenhausen again. I knew that Urs lived with friends when he was in Frankfurt. An undamaged house in the West End. I rang the bell. Urs wasn't there, nor his friends whom I knew from before. But a dentist had an office in the house and he let me in, saying that Urs was in Frankfurt but not home. I could wait in his place until Urs came back. I had waited patiently almost four years, here it was only an hour. But waiting was hard for me now.

Then Urs came, emaciated, astonished, and overjoyed at my return. He was shaken, I, too. After a very short time, the certainty: we belong together, want to stay together.

The ruins? They suited me, not only the German cities had been ruined by the war, I had been, too.

From Frankfurt I traveled to Munich—Munich, my home town, just had to—and sat together with four young Jews from the east. They spoke to me in Yiddish and when I said I didn't understand them there was a lot of whispering.

This much I had understood anyway: they wanted to buy cigarettes from me. I shook my head and said: "Give them." But they didn't want that and so a game began, they stuck the money in my pocket, I gave it back and they pushed it at me again. One could speak a little German: "Not a Jew?" "Yes, yes." "Are Jew and don't understand Yiddish?" "No." "What speak at home?" "German," I said, puzzled. But they shook their heads and didn't quite believe me.

There we sat, five who had come through alive. *Displaced persons.* Five human beings who had a similar fate and yet so different. Four who had been so kicked around by life that they would not accept cigarettes as a gift. I almost cried.

The second time I traveled back to Germany was the summer of 1948.

Urs had sent me two letters, one from the Mayor of Darmstadt, who said he had nothing against my coming, the other from the American Cultural Officer in Wiesbaden with similar contents. With the letters I traveled to American administrative headquarters in the Hague and did not get a visa. "Discussion with friends" did not constitute a satisfactory reason for travel. Was that the freedom that we had dreamed about for four long years? Had we imagined things backward? Were we now, without nationality, second-class citizens again? I wanted to go to Germany and I got to Germany, despite a lot of obstacles. Being illegal had taught me a lot. If you don't get what you want, take it however you can. Just so it's not criminal or harmful to others.

I had stationery printed with the address of a Doctor Müller in Odenwaldstrasse in Darmstadt. Was there really an Odenwaldstrasse? Well, it would seem likely. A little self-confidence. On the stationery I had a physician friend (his name was Müller, too) certify (doctor-language, couldn't be any mistakes with the diagnosis) that my sister in Darmstadt (I didn't have one) was critically ill and my presence was urgently needed. I couldn't go to the Americans in the Hague a second time.

So I got a transit visa for Germany, which was easy to obtain, and went to Switzerland.

The American officer in Bern was friendly and cooperative. Told me I would get the visa for sure. But it would take about ten days. I got scared, in ten days a lot of inquiries could be made. "Can't it be hurried up?" "If you pay 60 rappen, we'll send it special delivery." I paid and at ten o'clock the next morning in Zürich I had my passport with a visa.

Almost forty years have gone by since then, I travel with a genuine, German passport, anywhere I want to go. Do I still want to travel? I don't know. Often a violent longing for the Mediterranean, but also fear of the exertion, the changed surroundings. And, besides, the realization: I can no longer be anywhere where there is no hospital that is bearable for Europeans.

New experiences: age, illness. Which predominates? I'm inclined to say: illness. It has suddenly, from one hour to the next, made me incapable of many things.

Very many thoughts (very many more than earlier) about omnipresent death.

Since my brother died, I have had the feeling that part of me has also died.

I noticed it for the first time at the funeral, in front of the large, brown coffin. In this coffin lay a part of me as well, something that was now no more. My family no longer existed. I was, am, the last one. For my brother's ninetieth birthday celebration, which I couldn't attend because I was still not fully recovered, I had sent him a quotation from a poem by Musil called "Isis and Osiris": "Among a hundred brothers, this one, and I ate his heart and he mine." This piece of my heart that was now being cremated with him.

Often I think to myself: if I were to die the so-called "beautiful" death, suddenly fall over from a heart attack without knowing it—perhaps just a moment of searing pain and: now it's over—I would not even be able to have the liberating thought that I was dying before the atom bombs fell, before Jews were being killed again just because they were Jews, before our beautiful earth was completely destroyed. . . . Nothing, I'd get nothing more out of it than the fact that those close to me would be able to say: at least I'd been saved a lot of suffering. When was I ever one for saving, I who always wanted to spend everything? Wouldn't it be better to know, while suffering, that the end was coming and let out all of your feelings again, think all of your thoughts once more?

This fear of pain, as if the physical one were worse than the psychological.

I can't choose for myself; eighty years old, buffeted by illness, I know that one way or another it will soon end. One way or another, there is a solution for everything, my father (a model) wrote me that in his last letter, in which he felt sick, without yet being sick. And I should take it to heart, which I have always done, but can't any longer. Because the little bit of courage, the wish to pass through the unavoidable, dark, narrow gate as a "soldier and brave" is no longer as strong as before the illness.

In a hospital, a doctor who walks up to my bed, sees my hearing aid lying on the night table: "Oh, my," he says, "what all you don't need when you're old." Oh, my.

In Erika Mann's letters is told the story, which I find very moving, of how the nursemaid scolds the youngest son of von Hofmannsthal: "A boy of your age doesn't do that." The answer: "I am not a boy of my age, I am Raimund Hofmanns-thal." Am I not a woman of my age because I am the one uninterchangeable person who still writes, often still drives her automobile, and sometimes still thinks?

Naturally I am an eighty-year-old woman, one who has been severely ill, and nothing more. Everything else—illusion.

I, MICHAL, have had a very restless night. Many noises that I could not identify. My ears have become bad in my old age, I do not know whether that which I think I hear is real. That heightens the fear that I continuously feel here, in Solomon's palace, near Bathsheba. My fears, gigantic, when I cannot locate the source of the indistinct noises with my eyes. Thus I heard, or believe I heard: footsteps, talking, laughter. And suddenly, in the midst of my fear, I am overwhelmed by my recollections of the story, the worst that I experienced with David. Then the noises die away, all I hear now is rustling, without knowing whether it is really a rustling.

Simultaneously with the rustling comes a breath of cool air and drives away the sticky warmth of the night. Then I know for sure: it is raining. We have waited so long for the rain. I call my maidservant because I want to share the joy with another human. She comes, squats down before me. I stroke her beautiful, soft hair.

"It is raining, Princess." "Yes, it is raining, thanks be to Jahwe. You have never lived through such a drought before?" "None that lasted so long."

"We had not been living in Yerushalayim very long when there was one that lasted much longer. Month after month, not a drop of rain. Three long years. All the brooks and rivers had dried up, the cattle fell over in the meadows. But it was worst of all for the little children. The mothers could no longer nourish them, no milk came from their breasts.

"Many old people died as well, shriveled away to skeletons.

"How was an old person to obtain food? One had to go to the farmers, give them gold and linen in exchange. For the old ones, the road was too difficult."

"Did you have to go hungry, Princess?"

"No, not exactly, the king still had a few things given to him and gave us something from his abundance. But things were such that in the end he, too, could no longer think of anything but eating, of the two or three pieces of bread that still remained."

"And the king?" "Was as if he had turned to stone. But conjure up rain, even he could not do that."

"It is not yet so bad," says the maid.

"Now everything will be better. I know from those days that a single, strong rain will bring great relief."

"And now it has been raining for hours, Princess, we will not have to go hungry."

"Surely not, my little one."

Then I fall silent. I can tell my maidservant about the superficialities, but not about what really happened.

I often had the feeling then that all the joy of living, all the energy had left David. He quarreled with his God, asking: Why us?

He was also tortured by doubt as to whether his throne was really so secure as long as Saul's descendants were still alive. He never said it, not to me, Saul's daughter, but I knew him well enough to realize what was going on within him.

One day he went alone to the tent where the ark was kept. When he returned, he was very pale. He came into the rooms where Abigail and I lived, ate a little, but remained silent.

On the following day he had disappeared from the city. It was not until three days later that we saw him again. He appeared more serious than ever before.

"Jahwe has proclaimed to me," he began, "that the disgrace of murder lies upon Israel. You know that the Gibeonites do not actually belong to the children of Israel, they are descended from the Amorites. Saul once swore to protect them. But he broke his oath and let loose a bloodbath among them. For that Jahwe demands atonement."

"For the misdeed of a man who is already long dead?" asks Abigail.

"And the Gibeonites? Do they also demand atonement?"

David stares at the wall and shrugs his shoulders.

"I have been to see them, have offered them gold and herds so that Israel might be absolved. But they did not want treasure, they wanted blood. They demand seven of Saul's male descendants. With their deaths the debt would be canceled."

Seven—the holy number, dear to all of us. I ask quietly: "And you? Do believe so, too?"

"What should I do other than hand over the seven?"

"No!" screams Abigail, "that you cannot do."

"I must."

"Who?" I ask and am afraid of the answer.

"Not Mephibosheth. The son of Jonathan, my friend, will live."

"Who? Say who."

"Merab's five sons."

"No!" I scream, although I have never loved my sister. Five sons, five sons.

"And two sons of Saul's concubine Rizpah."

"No, no, Rizpah is my friend."

"I cannot take into consideration with whom you are friends."

"Would you have my son killed as well?"

"Not if he were my own. A son of another—perhaps."

It is the first time that he mentions Palti.

"I have no son."

"Be happy. I must do it, I must save my people. Just look around out there. In any case I cannot look upon one more dying child."

Abigail kneels down before David and puts the blue tassels of his coat to her mouth.

"Don't do it, don't do it. Say no."

"I have said yes, Abigail, I cannot go back. A king dare not break his word again."

We plead and beg and haggle with him the whole day.

I have the premonition that the demand of the Gibeonites is not entirely unwelcome to him. He fears the Saulists.

Abigail weeps, weeps the entire day.

It is the first time that her shining hero loses some of his gleam.

"The Gibeonites are only human, too," I say harshly, "what will happen if Jahwe does not send rain?"

"He will send it," says David.

And it came to pass, after the seven had been executed, that the rains came.

Jahwe? Not Jahwe? I wanted to know nothing of this man-destroying God and nothing of the king who served him in this way.

The descendants of Saul died and I could not forget that I was one of them.

I felt even closer to Abigail than before. About the hours in which we had pleaded with David for the lives of the Saulists we never spoke again.

One day around noontime I go to her, she who is always up is lying on her bed, clad in a bright red garment. Smiles when she sees me, but the smile disappears again immediately. She whispers: "It hurts, it stabs, here," and points to her heart. Her face is damp with perspiration. When I put my hand on her forehead I feel a moist cold instead of the expected heat.

I call a servant, order her to fetch the physician. He, a man no longer young but not yet old, with white threads showing through his black beard, listens to Abigail's breathing, lifts her eyelids, observes her pupils, and says reassuringly to her: "A slight indisposition. That will soon pass. But the princess must remain in bed, she may not move around, nor eat anything heavy."

She lies back, complains softly that she feels sick. But the physician has already gone, he does not hear her. I stay sitting beside her, hold her hand. We both remain silent. She is probably too weak to even speak. Then her lips move, with my ear quite close to her mouth, I understand that she is saying "thirsty."

I bring her the juice of pressed grapes. I know that she likes it. She sits up quickly, reaches eagerly for the cup that I hold out to her. Then her head falls to the side, her hand drops. A new, strange expression has come over her face, as if a large hand had wiped away all her sweetness, all her goodness, all her wisdom. Her eyes are wide open, her lids unblinking.

Then I know that she is dead. I scream, servant girls come running. I close Abigail's eyes, now she is lying there pale as marble. The physician summoned by the servants lays his head against her breast. "Yes, she is dead. We must summon the king." Naturally, this death means something to David. He, too, loved Abigail.

Shortly thereafter he is there, without retinue, alone.

Kneels before the bed, lays his face against hers, sheds a few tears. Not in despair, more in astonishment that this Jahwe who has granted him everything has taken from him something that he would like to have kept.

He has taken more from me, but I do not stand in such favor with him.

David arises, takes my hand, presses it to his lips and says seriously: "I loved Abigail very much. But when Jahwe takes a person from us, he does not do it without reason, we must submit to it and go on doing our duty. He, the Eternal One, has deprived us of a person, in his great goodness he will send another one to us."

Not to me, I want to shriek, but I do not get out a single word. I collapse, sobbing.

And just as Jahwe sent rain after the death of the followers of Saul, now he sent David a new person, a new wife. And if David is called, as often happens, "the Great," one should not forget the good fortune that never deserted him until just before his end.

Did his gifts, his good fortune make him great?

Although it is not given to us mortals to know whether something is our salvation or our destruction, David never doubted that everything was meant for his good fortune.

He had lost Abigail and demanded of Jahwe a new human being. Whether Jahwe granted it to him I do not know. But David knew. Abigail, the once-loved wife, was dead, a new wife came, more beautiful, younger—Bathsheba.

SOON AFTER Abigail's death, early in the summer, David invites me to eat supper with him. He has a delicious meal set before me, a choice wine as well, eats with me, then says it is too warm for him inside the house, he will rest a while on his roof.

When he returns, he is changed, excited, so that I ask him what has happened. He puts his arm around my shoulders and says, talking over me as if I were not present:

"I saw the most beautiful woman a few moments ago."

"Saw? Only saw?"

"She lives quite near, right down there, and bathed on her roof."

"On her roof, at full moon? So close to the palace? She wanted to be seen by you."

"How was she to know that I would be there, on my roof? Do not always think the worst immediately, dear Michal."

He is as trusting as a child when a woman pleases him. And this one is pleasing to him beyond all measure.

He sends a servant out to inquire who she is. He soon comes back and announces: "It is Bathsheba, wife of Uriah the Hittite who, under Joab's command, is besieging the Ammonite city of Rabbah."

"The wife of Uriah," says David disappointedly. "What a shame."

Immediately afterward, however, he commands his servant to fetch the woman. "Order of the king," he says, "that will make it easier for her."

And she comes after a good, long while. Has adorned herself, stands there in a garment of gold thread that reveals her beautiful body most advantageously.

"That is Michal," says David, "one of my earlier wives."

Her gaze strikes me like a poisoned arrow. I take my leave and know what will happen even before I am in my rooms.

Where was Abigail? From the first moment on I longed for someone who would protect me from Bathsheba. But there was no one.

Some time later, two or three months had passed, David sends for me again.

Bathsheba is there, her hair beautifully arranged, very pretty and self-confident. Already the mistress of this palace.

David pushes a stool over to me. Now we are sitting in a half-circle, all three.

"Michal," says David without being indirect. "Bathsheba is pregnant. You know what adultery means in our land."

I nod, because I know: stoning. Regardless of the person involved. Bathsheba cries, hides her face in her hands. Nothing more is left of her assurance.

"Be calm, my darling," says David comfortingly and strokes her hair. "We will find something to tell the people."

I think hard, quickly, then I interject: "Send a messenger to Joab, command him to send Uriah home. If he sleeps here with Bathsheba, the child she bears will be his, as far as he and the whole world will know."

"My clever Michal," says David. "The daughter of a king always has good advice." At this moment he is close to me and loves me again for the first time in a long while.

Why am I the very one who has tried to save Bathsheba? Although I know immediately that she will never forgive me for it. Certainly not because I have seen her weak and helpless.

Is it pity for this miserable, trembling, tearful creature? And I know also that being stoned is a slow, terrible death. Perhaps there is even a little bit of vanity as well and the joy of doing something for David.

I do not want to make myself better than I am. I also did not want her and David to have a child together.

Only a few days had passed before Uriah arrived, proud to have been summoned by his king. A coarse, strutting rooster.

David knew how to deal with soldiers. He entertained his guest in the palace, asked him this and that about the siege of the city and the mood of the troops, gave him so much strong wine that the man was soon intoxicated. At the end of the evening David said (he related everything to me exactly): "You are a brave fellow. I wish all of my warriors were like you. You have earned a reward. And now go home to your wife."

But Uriah did not go. Lay down at the entrance to the palace beside David's bodyguards.

On the following evening, the same thing. "Why do you not go home?" asked David impatiently.

"My king has already bestowed too much honor upon me. I do not wish to be better treated than my comrades who are sleeping out in the open before Rabbah."

There was nothing to be done. Perhaps this aggravating yokel sensed that he was being misused in some nasty business. Perhaps he did not want to sleep with any woman. Had never done it, there is such a thing, such things happen, and the wretched Bathsheba had just kept quiet about it.

After the failed attempt with Uriah, David comes to me, downcast, near desperation.

"Your plan, Michal, was good, but Uriah is a simpleton and has not slept with Bathsheba. Not that it would have been a pleasant thought for me, knowing that she was in the arms of another man. Well, I could have spared myself these unpleasant feelings. I cannot just treat him like a male dog that one sets on a bitch in heat. We have another plan now. I will send Uriah back and have him carry a message to Joab that he should keep Uriah in the forefront of the battle until he is killed."

It takes my breath away. "David," I say harshly, "you have not thought that up by yourself."

He does not even try to contradict me, just lowers his lids with their long lashes and does not look at me.

"It has to be," he says softly. "I could not bear it if they were to stone Bathsheba. And it is not even certain that they would not stone me as well." Then resolutely and proudly. "Israel needs me. I do not have the right to forsake my mission because of this unhappy affair."

I realize with horror that he is conscious of the sin and is afraid that Jahwe will not forgive him for it. His clean hands, unsullied by blood. That is all past now, now and for all time.

Forever will the name Uriah cast a shadow upon the name David.

He soon goes away and leaves me behind in despair. I will share in the guilt of Uriah's death and I hate not only myself, but also David and Bathsheba.

What I had wanted: to foist off on a man a child sired by someone else, that was not really so bad, that often happened, but to send a man away with his own death warrant, that could not be allowed.

Oh this woman who befouled everything. I loathed her. This loathing has never passed away.

After just a few days she received the news that her husband had fallen in battle.

Cries of lamentation resounded from her house where, with the door wide open so all could see, she was sitting on the floor with her garments torn to shreds and ashes strewn upon her head.

I was sick at the heart for Uriah, for David. And again David had Joab for a conspirator, was now even more in his power than before.

The affair did not remain a secret. Even before David brought Bathsheba to the palace as his wife after the period of mourning had elapsed, everyone knew the facts. Among David's servants or bodyguards there must have been someone who spread the story outside the walls.

Nathan had made it known to David that he wanted to speak to him and, moreover, in my house. Why I should be present I do not know.

And so they both come to me, Nathan, the prophet, with a very serious expression, David quiet and with downcast eyes.

Nathan arranges himself comfortably, then he says: "Judge

David, I would like to present to you a case in which I am having difficulty pronouncing judgment. Your opinion will be decisive. Hear me then:

"Once upon a time there lived in the same country, not far apart from one another, a very rich man and a very poor man. The poor man possessed a single little lamb which he loved, cherished, and looked after like his own child. The rich man, on the other hand, possessed great flocks of lambs.

"One day the rich man received an important visitor or at least a visitor whom he considered important for the increase of his riches.

"And he wanted to set before this visitor a splendid meal. Since none of his own lambs appeared good enough to him, he had the lamb of the poor man slaughtered and served it to his guest.

"Now I ask you, David, the Judge, what should happen to the rich man?"

David has listened with interest as befits a judge to whom two parties are presenting their case.

But he has not understood what Nathan was driving at.

I, on the other hand, comprehend immediately. The parable pleases me, only I do not like the fact that Bathsheba is being compared to a little lamb.

Impatiently, Nathan repeats his question: "Judge David, what should happen to the rich man?"

"He has behaved despicably," says David quickly. "He deserves death."

Nathan straightens up and says harshly without the least hesitation in his voice: "You, yourself, are that man. But the Eternal One, in his goodness, does not yet wish your death. But the fruit of sin, the child that Bathsheba will bring into the world, will not remain alive."

•

Last night, I, Michal, dreamed of Jonathan. Of Jonathan and Absalom, and they both were one. This one wanted to take me with him on a long journey. He came riding upon a horse and the horse was Eran. I wanted to climb on behind the rider and could not get up. Screamed: I cannot, am too old. The rider (and now it was quite distinctly Jonathan) turned around and said: You can. Of course you can. He bent down to me and pulled me up. I sat behind him as I did long ago and held on to him tightly. His dark hair blew in my face. But it was not Jonathan's, it was Absalom's hair. Thicker than I had ever seen on a person before. And it exuded all the fragrances that I knew. We rode quickly, to a place unknown to me, and suddenly were surrounded by many people. But they were not people of flesh and blood, they were shadows, wraiths through whom I could see. Then I knew we were in Sheol, the netherworld. So I was dead, dead like Jonathan and Absalom. But I was not sad, only happy to be with them. But the strange thing was that I felt no love for them any longer. Even love was dead. I cried out softly and awakened.

Since Abigail was dead and Bathsheba was living in the palace, I sought new friendship. I did not find it with Maacha, the shy, the prudish one. She, too, lived close to me, I often went into her house, where it smelled of the herbs and spices that hung from the ceiling. Most of the time she had a large iron pot on the fire, in which she stirred around with a long branch from which the bark had been stripped. All the while she murmured incantations or sang softly to herself. It was said that she was a sorceress and the more often I saw her, the more I believed it.

Had she once brewed a love potion for David? Often I attempted to imagine how it had been when she made love to him, but I did not succeed. However it was, he had two children by her, the most beautiful children I knew.

As a child, Tamar was just as reserved as her mother, I never succeeded in breaking through her shyness. With Absalom that was not difficult. He snuggled up to me and called me "my little mother." Maacha would frown angrily then. He knew as well as I that she did not like that.

She believed in ghosts and had passed on something of this belief to Absalom.

"Michal," he would say, "Mother, you may not leave town today, it is not a good day." "When will it be a good day, Absalom?" He smiled slyly: "I do not know. You must ask Maacha, she knows." Or: "Do not go to David today. He could do you harm." "David will not harm me, Absalom. I was once his wife." And: "Mother, why do you not have a child?" "I just never had one, Absalom." "That doesn't matter, Mother, you have me. I don't like other children near me. Only Tamar, she may be there." Even then he loved his sister, who became his fate, and would caress her playfully.

"Little Mother, did you love David?"

"Yes, Absalom, very, very much."

"Was he handsome when he was young?" "Very handsome, Absalom."

Then quickly the question: "As handsome as I? Or even more handsome?"

To that I could not give an answer. Maacha said impatiently: "You should keep your mouth closed. Don't show off."

But you have me . . . sometimes I actually began to believe that he was my child. If I had been able to pray, I would have prayed for this child. It was a mistake, wrong, presumptuous, I know. He was not my child, but I forgot that he was not.

And had it not seemed sinful to me, I would have told Absalom not once, but a hundred times, how beautiful I found him. With his finely carved face, the gray eyes—David's eyes. With his lean boy's body, the well-formed muscles of his naked arms and legs. With his ingratiating voice that said "my little mother" to me.

Thus nothing came of my friendship with Maacha; she remained as distant to me as on the first day.

I, G R E T E , the late-born, the survivor who has not forgotten, cannot forget, and does not want to forget, can never see a small child holding its mother's hand and her tender, protective looks, without remembering with almost physical pain the mothers who, on the ramp of Auschwitz or some other camp, had their children torn from their arms and smashed against a wall or shot in front of their very eyes.

And once, still during the war, I said: adults, perhaps, but the Germans don't kill children.

The more time goes by, the greater the distance from it, the harder it is to comprehend all that.

Despite all or just because of it I go on thinking it through, not avoiding it, and am convinced, for the most part, that I have experienced all the horrors so often, so intensively, that nothing can rob me any longer of my laboriously acquired equanimity.

But then it happens to me anyway, I'm sitting in front of the television set and crying my eyes out.

It is a program commemorating the liberation of Auschwitz forty years ago. An old, very frail, well-dressed, distinguished woman is telling that she gave birth to a little girl in Auschwitz—even that is unimaginable. Then Mengele came the next day and ordered her to bind up her breasts, he wanted to know how long a newborn child could live without nourishment.

Human intellect that wants to know everything, wants to make everything, that thought up the atom bomb and tenderly called it "little boy," that invented Zyklon B, tanks, rockets, and airplanes with friendly names like Enola Gay, weapons that can transform the world into icy night and extinguish all life. And that thinks it is important to determine how long a babe in arms will stay alive without nourishment.

The mother tried to feed the child with bread she'd already chewed, she didn't have anything else. But it wasted away hour by hour and she had to watch it happen. Mengele came back, announced to her that she and the child would go to the gas chamber the next day. That night a woman doctor (a German?) gave her a syringe with morphine so that she could kill the child. She said: I can't. And the doctor: You must.

The next morning, Mengele asked about the child. It had died. His comment: You're lucky.

Right away I think: And this pig is alive. At the same time, I know that he is no longer alive, at least with probability that verges on certainty, that he is no longer alive, and conclude that this knowledge doesn't mean anything to me any more.

I'm indifferent. There are still enough like him who are destroying the world.

Don't tell me you would suffer from the atrocities just as I do. You have not lived through the horror year by year, day by day, awake and asleep.

In Claude Lanzmann's film *Shoah* a survivor of the Warsaw ghetto says: If you could lick my heart you would be poisoned.

So it is. Nothing in this world can free our hearts of this poison.

Again and again I am asked why I went back to Germany. It's my country, where my language is spoken. It remains my country, whether I like it or not (and very often I don't like it).

I'm German, well OK: a German Jew. In Paris, in the late 1920s, when I walked by, wearing French clothes, the newspaper boys yelled: *"Berliner Tageblatt, Vossiche Zeitung."*

Besides, I was discriminated against much earlier as a German than as a Jew. It was 1926, a few days after my twentieth birthday. My brother and I had put down our jackets to save two seats on the train from Brussels to Ostend and got off again.

Perhaps this way of reserving seats was not customary in Belgium, at any rate, when we came back, a man was standing there yelling insults at us and when he heard that we were speaking German, he started to scream: "Assassins, assassins."

We didn't answer back at all. Perhaps he had lost a son in the war, I would have liked to know because possibly I would have understood him better. It seemed monstrous to me to be labeled a murderer, without evidence, without a hearing.

A brother of my grandfather, a rich bachelor in America, had just died about this time and had expressly excluded us, his

German relatives, as heirs because his favorite nephew had been killed in the American army.

Collective guilt even then.

Rather early the realization of how painful it can be, to be stamped as something, to be on a list. It does not necessarily have to be a minority. A nation will do as well.

In 1946 I did not get a Norwegian visa, because my displaced person's passport contained the words "German-born."

My German identity was already clear to me soon after my return and I have never doubted it since then.

More difficult the question about my Jewish identity. A while ago, when a childhood friend who had emigrated and was living in Sweden asked on behalf of his daughter (the daughter: two Jewish parents, grown up without religion, considers herself a Swede) what Jewish identity was, I was evasive at first: I don't know. But I've thought about it a lot since then and am of the opinion that belief is necessary for Jewish identity, the belief in Jahwe, the God invented by the Jews and passed on to two world religions. After that, a bond with the Land of Israel, the feeling of a homeland in Eretz Israel, the land of our fathers. Neither the one nor the other is present in me, never was present, hence I never had a Jewish identity. What remains is that I have experienced, as a Jew, what suffering means.

So probably the single rudiment of an identity, mutual suffering and fate.

Family history? One of my forebears, a Franconian rabbi in the eighteenth century (his first name was David) published a thick book called Pardes David, the Garden of David. The book, printed in Hebrew, unintelligible to me, presumably Bible and Talmud commentaries, says nothing to me.

Have I become more Jewish since I've been involved with David and Michal? Yes, surely, something has started that was not there before.

A new theme in my life, new material, previously unknown to me. But why am I preoccupied with David?

Jewish roots, naturally. Also curiosity and the conjecture that not only the myths and history of the Greeks are worth knowing, but those of the Jews as well.

Despite the long preoccupation with David, I don't know much better than I did in the beginning what he was, what constituted the greatness that established his fame, which has lasted throughout three millennia.

That he was a murderer, among many other things, is certain. Also, that he possessed charisma, otherwise he would hardly have risen from shepherd to king. Did he resemble Michelangelo's David or Rembrandt's or neither of them? Did the two artists know more about him than I do? I don't believe so.

Do we, the late-born, really know anything at all about someone who lived in the past?

Always mere suppositions, speculations, always a tantalizing game, stone is laid against stone until the puzzle reveals a picture.

My stones: a charismatic murderer, a good musician, a good poet, a successful general, probably a good lover, a man whose blond hair and light skin were conspicuous in the midst of his people, a believer, visibly blessed by God.

And Michal, my heroine? What about her? No one could be occupied so intensively with a person without becoming fond of her.

For me, she was never a sister, like Antigone, admired and envied for her courage. No deep relationship between me and this woman who was pushed around and often misused by men. Only sympathy and compassion for one who had to live at the beginning of time, when everything was still in flux; in the chaos in which there was no such thing as justice or injustice, she had to make decisions, take sides, and cling to a difficult life that was threatened from all sides.

She and I, bound together by our belonging to a people that is not really one people at all but always wanted to be one: two Jewish women.

She, Michal, was the vessel into which I could pour my thoughts, my wishes, and that which seemed reasonable to me and she was a good vessel for me. For that may she be thanked across all time.

THE WEATHER is gloomy this spring. It rains, rains. But still much better than the great drought. I, Michal, like to listen to the raindrops, it is a good sound that promises a fruitful harvest. Yet when there is no sun to brighten the world, the gloomy thoughts come and I remember all the bitterness that I experienced here.

There was Tamar, Absalom's sister, who became more and more charming. As shy as her mother and playfully happy like a little animal that one would like to take in one's arms and caress.

David loved both children, but he no longer doted so blindly on Absalom.

Many times I thought that there was no longer any room in his heart beside Bathsheba, whom he adored.

Her child, a little son, came into the world, and after a few weeks of pitiful existence, became seriously ill.

David prayed, fasted, slept on the hard ground, spoke with no one.

After several days the little boy died and no one could bring himself to inform David. More than once he had had bearers of bad tidings put to death.

"I will tell him," I say to Benaiah, the leader of the Cherethites and Pelethites. "He will not do anything to me."

He is sitting on the floor when I enter his room and greet him softly: "Shalom, David."

He lifts his head, looks at me out of reddened eyes. An aging man. I notice it for the first time. Then he stammers: "The child is dead, it is so, Michal?"

"Yes, David, the child is dead."

A few tears run down his cheeks. But then he calls a servant and bids him bring fresh clothing and something to eat.

Astonished, I say: "You fasted while the child was sick, now that he is dead, you demand something to eat?"

"Why should I go on fasting?" His voice sounds curiously cool. "Jahwe has taken the child from me. Not even he can give him back. He has not heard my prayers, has not accepted my fasting as penance."

That is David's bright, clear reasoning. I love him very much at this moment.

It is strange: we are a couple and yet not a couple.

Often the old love flares up in one of us, but it does not have enough strength to ignite something that will no longer burn.

I believe that he often feels protected as long as I am near him. We do not come closer to one another, we do not get free of one another. Since I learned that Palti was dead, there has been no one in whose presence I would have preferred to live.

Tamar's misfortune caused yet another deep rift between us. I could not forgive him for having sent her to Amnon. He loved his family and yet his mind was too much occupied with the affairs of state for him to have been able to judge his children correctly.

Only Bathsheba's child, Solomon, the son she brought into the world one year after the death of her firstborn, remained a stranger to him. That precocious, conceited, unlikable boy possessed by learning, who never played, became David's successor.

David also loved Amnon, his eldest. A squat, crude, companionable sort, thus had Abner described him to me once, on the way to Hebron, and that he actually was.

Amnon had had a hard youth, was the child of the fugitive, the robber, David, had starved and shivered with David, had shifted from one hiding place to another.

Tamar was not only beautiful, she was also gifted. A graceful dancer with a beautiful voice. Many of the bright little carpets in my rooms had been woven for me by her. She baked the best fig cakes that I knew of. She liked to laugh, made fun of many things, and, when I visited her, she danced for us, for her mother, Absalom, and me.

Absalom watched her, entranced, and I often thought that Jonathan's and my love was repeating itself with these two. Would such a terrible thing not have happened without this love? An idle question and yet a shadow hung over them both from the very beginning. Maacha noticed it as well, occasionally she said something that hinted at it, but she could not conjure it away.

One day I was accompanying Tamar to the palace. On the way back we met Amnon, who walked past us with a curt greeting. I turned around after him, and then I saw that he had also turned around, saw his desirous gaze. Not Tamar, I thought, shocked.

But my maidservants, who reported all the gossip in Yerushalayim to me, told me that at the well people were saying that Prince Amnon was in love with his half-sister Tamar and intended to ask David for her hand. That was not common but not completely impossible either, under certain circumstances our laws permitted marriage between a man and his half-sister.

I did not see David very often at this time, but one time he came to me with a troubled expression.

"Amnon is ill, severely ill," he said and I nodded, it was a matter of indifference to me whether Amnon was sick or healthy.

David was troubled about it: "I have lost my little son, it would be unbearable for me now, to see the eldest one waste away."

"Is it that bad?"

"Very bad. He has fever, cannot eat or sleep."

"Well, now," I said, "he's not going to die right away because of that." "I have been with him," said David, "and have begged him to eat something just for my sake."

"Did he do it?"

He shook his head sadly: "No, but he promised that if Tamar would come to him and make her heart-shaped bread in his presence, he would take two pieces of it, nothing more."

"Tamar cannot go to him, that is impossible," I said firmly.

"Why ever not? I have just come from her and have bidden her to prepare the bread."

"That dare not happen."

"Why not? She is his sister."

"Whom he loves."

"It is better to love a sister than to hate her."

I said nothing more. He did not understand me. I should have explained to him that Amnon desired his sister, that he was unrestrained in his desire, just like his father. Thus I remained silent at the moment when I should have spoken and let fate take its course. Silence as guilt. Again did not say no. Why?

Maacha and Absalom let Tamar go as well. And she herself had wanted to.

When I saw her again, I do not like to think about it, but she belongs in my story, when I saw her again on the next day, Absalom had come for me, Tamar was crouching in a dark corner, pale, trembling, her pretty face distorted by hate.

The bright, hooded cloak, which only the virgins of the royal house were permitted to wear, was torn or actually cut to shreds, Tamar was still holding in her hand the knife with which she had done the work of destruction. She had covered her head with ashes and was crying, crying as I have never seen a human being cry. Maacha was sitting motionlessly on a stool. Absalom it was, who told me what had happened.

Tamar had gone to Amnon and, in a side room, but in a way that he could see her from his bed, had been braiding the dough into heart shapes. There was still a servant present who was to bring the bread to Amnon. But he had sent the servant away so that Tamar herself had to bring it to him. As she stood at the side of his bed, he said that he loved her, desired her, she should lie down with him, now, on the spot. She resisted, then he raised himself up, threw his arms around her and pulled her down to him. She fought with him, screamed, but he was the stronger of the two, and then he took her by force. "He has violated her, that brutal pig," Absalom said. "He has robbed her for all time of any possibility of having a husband."

But the story did not end with the rape. Scarcely had he possessed her, when his love was transformed into hate. Also, he had noticed spots of blood on his bed, probably was revolted by them.

He raised a great outcry and ordered the servants who had rushed in (one of them had reported about the bloodstains) to throw out this whore who had thrown herself at him in such an unchaste way. Which then happened.

I run over to the palace to speak with David. To me, that appeared to be necessary above all. But I do not succeed in speaking with him alone. Bathsheba is with him and so I must tell Tamar's story in her presence. She laughs: "Such a to-do, probably she seduced him and is now turning everything around."

I have the desire to strike her, but since I do not want to do that in front of David, I just say to him: "Go and look at your child Tamar for yourself."

David has become pale, his forehead looks blotchy.

I demand: "You must punish Amnon."

"Such presumption," whines Bathsheba. "We only know what happened from the reports of that crazy girl. The king cannot really punish the crown prince based on a mere rumor." Why was she standing up for Amnon? She probably feared him less than Absalom, whom the people loved. Was she already looking out for Solomon's future?

It was the first, but not the last time that she interfered with affairs of state or family in my presence. Her power over David was so great that he did not attempt anything. He did not punish Amnon, he did not go to Tamar and did not see her in her frightful condition. She was like a suddenly extinguished light. Her grace, her irony, her love of dancing—all gone. A wretched creature that cried when one spoke to her, crouched in darkened rooms, and tore to shreds every garment that Maacha put on her.

Time brought about no change in Tamar's condition. She remained a dishonored lunatic as long as she lived. Absalom saw to her every day, surrounded her with love and tenderness, but even that could do nothing.

Maacha had turned away from me. She spoke with her children, but never to me, I had not succeeded in getting the king to punish Amnon, thus I had become part of David for her and she despised everything that had to do with David.

Absalom never again spoke to Amnon, not for two years. They met at family celebrations and ceremonies of state. But Absalom acted as if he did not see his brother.

No one seemed to be frightened by it. Was I the only one who noticed Absalom's hatred? I knew that one day he would avenge Tamar and I trembled at the thought.

Absalom possessed large stretches of land in the northern part of Yerushalayim. He was often there nowadays; sometimes he took Maacha, Tamar, and me, as well, out there along with him.

Two years had passed when he told me that he wanted to hold festivities at the time of sheepshearing. He wanted to invite his brothers and also David.

"And Tamar?" I asked anxiously. He laughed: "Tamar will be there. The queen of the festival."

I looked at him worriedly. His brow was wrinkled. In his eyes there was still hatred.

I tried to talk him out of the festival, above all, having Tamar there.

"Do you want to invite Amnon also?" I asked.

"Naturally."

"And Tamar will see him?"

"It does not matter to me that Tamar sees him, but that he sees Tamar."

I took his hand: "Tamar could become even sicker if she sees him."

He laughed: "Even sicker? Tamar could die and that would only be good."

"Is that why you want to?"

"No, that is not why."

I said nothing more. Yet I knew now that he was planning something terrible. A fratricide? A fratricide stands at the beginning of history, when Cain struck down Abel, a fratricide will very possibly be the last thing at the end. And is not every murder basically a fratricide?

After a few days I saw Absalom again and he said disappointedly: "Father is not coming." "And Amnon?" "Coming. David has given his express permission."

Me he did not invite and that made me even more suspicious.

On the day of the festival I remained in Yerushalayim and listened, full of fear, to the sounds that penetrated to me from outside. But for many, many hours, everything remained quiet.

Not until evening did I hear noises and many footsteps approaching the palace.

I asked my chambermaid: "What is happening?" "Prince Absalom has killed all the king's sons." "All?" I asked in disbelief and noticed how my heart was racing. "All."

When dawn came on the following morning and over the Mount of Olives hung the first golden clouds whose color soon shaded off to a delicate pink, I did not want to remain at home any longer. Go to Maacha? There was no sense to that, with her reserve she would only plunge me into greater agitation.

To David? Bathsheba was there and could only be over-joyed that, aside from Solomon and Absalom who had become his brothers' murderer, there were no more sons of David.

And so I stood there and looked toward the rising sun. Then I saw that a procession was coming down from the Mount of Olives, riders on asses and mules, and at the head of them rode Adonijah who came after Amnon in the order of successors to the throne.

I let the column pass by, but Amnon was not among them.

Amnon was dead. I soon heard that from the people who were running around in the streets. Absalom had killed him or had had him killed by his men.

That Amnon had gotten what he deserved was what every-one felt and the people probably still loved Absalom. But what would David do?

I made my way through the throngs of people, then through an alley to the palace.

I was admitted immediately. To my relief, I found him alone, without Bathsheba.

David was sitting bent over deeply, his head buried in his hands. Actually I had expected that he would be weeping for Absalom, even if his love for him had no longer been so visible recently. But he was weeping and mourning for Amnon.

I put my hand on his shoulder. "Did you love Amnon, David?"

He lifted his head: "Amnon was my child, my eldest. A father loves his children."

His grief, his despair were genuine. Of Absalom, he said nothing. Did not even ask where he was.

I could not have told him at this moment. Only later did I hear it from Maacha. He had fled to his grandfather, the King of Geshur, and would remain there. Maacha found that which had happened entirely right and proper. For her, blood revenge went without saying.

Tamar had not been there at Amnon's death, a sympathetic servant had previously led her to a chamber where she could remain alone.

Now, however, at home again in Yerushalayim, she wept and longed for her brother and no one could help her.

⸱⸝⸜ *W*HENEVER I, Grete, turn on the evening news on television, Shagi sits down in front of the door to the hallway and whines softly. She does not like strange voices in the room without being able to see or smell the person speaking.

Once the news is over, I get her from the hall where her basket is kept and bring her to my—to our bedroom. And say at the same time: "Beddy," a word that gets her up on her feet right away. She does not jump onto the bed, but crawls under it. The springs almost reach to the floor, that doesn't disturb her, quite the opposite. She creeps between them and lies happily in the farthest left corner, protected by two walls.

I don't go to her for the longest time today. On television they're showing a film titled *Nathan–Shylock,* which is supposed to show the good Jew beside the bad one. I stay up late till the end, only because they're showing Kortner as Shylock in many of the scenes (an old version that I've seen already).

For that, I, an early-to-bed person, would even stay up the whole night. We will not see the likes of him again.

With this joy there is also a lot of sadness. Sadness as always, when it's about something Jewish. Strangely enough: I feel at home with his monologue, which is declaimed with extraordinary musicality, like an aria. "I am a Jew. Does not a Jew have hands, limbs, organs, senses, affections, passions? Nourished with the same food, wounded by the same weapons, subject to the same illnesses, healed by the same means, formed, warmed, and chilled by the very same winter and summer as a Christian? If you stab us, do we not bleed? If you tickle us, do we not laugh? If you poison us, do we not die? If you insult us, shall we not seek revenge? If we are so similar to you in all things, then we will do as you do in this also. If a Jew insults a Christian, what is his humility? Revenge!" Kortner ends with the voluptuous scream, re-e-venge, which he starts like a tenor hitting high C.

No one around me has ever talked and acted like a caricature of a Jew and he does it incredibly. I don't know what strikes me as so familiar, don't know, either, why the re-e-venge, during which he plays with his body like he's playing with a ball, should excite me so. At the same time, revenge is a feeling that I don't know, don't want to know. It has to be something elementally Jewish, elementally mythical.

Shylock, the poor guy for whom everything goes wrong. The bad Jew? No, he is not bad, only pitiable because the means for his re-e-venge are so incredibly limited.

I am very tired when I go to my bedroom after midnight. The bed is empty, Shagi is still lying underneath.

In spite of my excitement, I soon fall asleep.

Am awake again at three. My left hand feels around toward my feet. At the level of the bend of my knees, between me and the wall, Shagi is lying. I did not notice when she jumped up, light as a feather, and lay down there. I feel for her, take her tousle-head in my hand and pet her. She likes that.

Only in the morning, when it's starting to get light outside, will she crawl up to me and get her hair all over my face, until I say: "That's enough, now, beat it!"

Naturally she noticed during the night that I was more restless than usual, but didn't understand.

What can she really understand of this puzzle—a human being? Even if it's her human, which she surely knows, the one who pets her most often, most tenderly, who feeds her, the one she runs after, wherever it goes. I sit up, stay in bed, propped on one arm, and begin to tell Shagi softly:

"Your human is a Jew, and that means an extra measure of sorrow."

She cocks her head sideways and looks at me with her big, intelligent eyes.

What distinguishes dogs from all other living things is that you can talk to them as if you were talking to yourself.

"When I got sick, Shagi, you had only been with me for two months, but despite that, my being away bothered you. When I came home from the hospital, excited and happy to finally see you again, you treated me with contempt because I had gone away from you.

"I am old, dearly beloved, and someday not too far away I will have to leave you, then you'll have to find a new human, with your charm and cheekiness, you'll succeed easily. With luck your new human will be younger and happier than I am, will run the legs off you and won't ever get tired of throwing sticks and balls for you as long as you want to. That I am happy so little has to do with my being Jewish. I drag too much horror around with me.

"They hunted for us, Shagi, the hunters didn't catch me, but the human who was the dearest of all to me, they imprisoned and killed him. Human beings are murderers, lucky for you, you don't know that and think they're all good.

"For some Central American country or other, for which I wanted a visa, I had to fill in the space marked 'race' on the questionnaire. I wasn't permitted to write 'human,' and not 'Jew,' either, I had to write 'white.' White is superior, they consider it something special. That's how dumb humans are.

"With regard to that, a great author, an 'Aryan,' wrote in those days when the hunt for us was still in full swing: 'For we are all made of the same substance and the same spirit as well. The godforsaken ones who deny that with despicable cruelty will not be forgiven.'

"That was too optimistic, neither in the lower nor in the upper ranks has judgment been passed on them.

"Do you see, dearly beloved, you have a sad human whose only joy is you. You didn't pick me out, actually I picked you from among your five sisters and brothers, because I liked your eyes best."

I stop talking to Shagi, I have to go on thinking alone.

Strange: even during the persecution I did not have the feeling that they could mean me. Each time I left the house I had to make it clear to myself again: I look Jewish, my (forged) identification card is not good enough so that they'll accept it. If I go out into the street, they'll stop me and send me to the east. (The east, our word in those days for Auschwitz and other camps which, with few exceptions, we did not know by name.)

Even when anti-Semitism flares up now, the same feeling that they don't mean me.

At the same time, my consciousness of bearing responsibility for all Jews is very strong. If I behave badly, all Jews behave badly. It was always that way and presumably it will never be otherwise.

Since my Jewish identity is so weak without belief in God or the feeling of a homeland in Israel, I think about what ties me to that which is Jewish and to Michal.

Thomas Mann, with whom the beautiful words about the godforsaken also originate, said in a speech about the problem of anti-Semitism in which he also described why he wrote *Joseph:* "The typical is always simultaneously the mythical."

And so I must climb deep down, into the dark reaches, and come to the realization that it is probably the mythical that has caused me to make Michal into the protagonist of my story.

꩜ *In* THE time after Amnon's death, it was as if a dark veil lay over us and the city.

The terrible word fratricide spoiled the world for us. No one could laugh as before.

I, Michal, lived in seclusion and longed for Absalom.

It was a different longing than that for Palti, Jonathan, Abigail. No matter how strong the yearning for the dead is, it eventually becomes calmer, settles down with time.

They do not come back and if they returned, they would find in us a different person than the one they left behind. Perhaps love would no longer be so strong then. The yearning for someone who is alive, however, never subsides as long as there is the possibility of seeing him again, it gnaws at us, hurts, torments.

I saw David almost never, imagined, however, that things were going for him as they were for me. Amnon was dead. But

Absalom was alive. Why did David not have him, once his favorite son, return home?

Curiously enough, because of David's marriage to Bathsheba, whom he loved passionately now as much as ever, his relationship with her grandfather Ahithophel was deeply disturbed. It may be that the old man held it against the king that the marriage had taken place without his consent, indeed, without his knowledge. And, naturally, he knew, as did everyone, the story of Uriah's death.

He himself, that wise man, perhaps would have had better advice than to send Uriah to his death with Joab's help. But what has happened has happened. Ahithophel, who disapproved of Bathsheba's influence on the affairs of state, withdrew from court, and David, who had other advisors, no longer called upon him.

And so three years passed. Absalom was still in Geshur and it looked as if he would stay there forever.

Then help came from a direction from which I would have least expected it—from Joab. I do not know why he, the butcher, who later murdered Absalom in cold blood despite David's strict orders, why he of all people wanted to have him back. May be that he held him to be the most suitable successor to David and that the welfare of the country came before everything else.

In any case, he noticed that David's grief for Amnon had subsided and, with it, his anger at Absalom.

One of David's trusted friends, Jacob, told me that Joab was making remarks now and again that it was getting to be time to let Absalom return home. But the king said no, each time no and his expression became gloomy.

I cannot let the matter rest. One evening I go to the palace, I make my way to David without hindrance and find him alone, slumped on his throne.

When he sees me, he smiles weakly: "Michal, my little Michal, what a joy to see you." I say softly: "You are still grieving for Amnon?" He shakes his head. "Not for Amnon, for Absalom. Amnon is dead, I could mourn for him and that I have done. But Absalom lives and yet I have lost him."

"One who is alive can be with us again one day."

He looks at me sadly: "I loved that son. Now every feeling for him has died away. Many times I wish that Amnon had killed him."

"He could be with us again, David, if you allowed him to come and if he did not have to fear for his life here."

"You think," he speaks very slowly and doubtfully, "that I should permit Joab to bring him home?"

"Yes, David. As quickly as possible."

"He may perhaps come back, but I do not wish to see him."

Absalom in Yerushalayim without David's seeing him: that strikes me as so devious that I do not know whether it is good to say yes to David's proposal.

It was not good, today I know that. If David had immediately allowed Absalom to be in his presence again, his son would probably have never risen against him.

We both remained silent awhile, deep in thought.

David looks at me questioningly and I notice how worn, how old he looks.

"You knew Absalom well, Michal, do you believe he wanted only to avenge the wrong that had been done to Tamar, or that he also wanted to get rid of the man who stood between him and the throne?"

There it is, the question that I ask myself over and over

again, that people still whisper to each other in the market-place, even now, after so long a time.

"It is true, David, I have known Absalom well. But who really knows the most secret thoughts of people, even those very close to us, especially when they are ambitious?"

"Have you never asked yourself that, Michal?"

"Very often, David, but I have not found an answer. I only know that he could not bear Tamar's rape."

"And because of that he had to kill his brother? Because of a girl?"

"Jonathan would have killed you, too, if you had raped me and defamed me afterward."

"Do you think so? But I would never have done such a thing."

"Tamar is your child too, David."

"Yes, a terrible thing happened to her and I have heard that her mind is still disturbed."

"And will be forever. Even her beauty is destroyed. She often looks like an old, old woman."

"Who knows whether she did not provoke him to the rape, that is said to happen with girls."

"That is Bathsheba's view, David."

"But just for that reason it could be right."

"It is not right. I knew Tamar as well as Absalom."

He turns away and that means that my audience is at an end. On the very next day, he orders Joab to fetch Absalom home.

It took a long time until he came. Geshur is far away.

During these days, I sat mostly with Maacha, who had slowly become somewhat more friendly in her reserved way.

All of a sudden, many voices in front of the house, the heavy tread of camels.

There is impatient knocking at the door, Maacha opens it and falls into her son's arms with a soft cry.

There he stands, surrounded by curious onlookers who stare at him admiringly, beaming, more handsome than ever, more mature, he has become a little heavier, with his incredibly thick hair, a foreign ruler, richly adorned with jewelry, which is rarely the custom with our men.

An angel of Jahwe, yes, but not one like David once was with his harp. Rather, one with the flaming sword, who judges and gives battle. He brings many beautiful pieces of jewelry along for us three women.

After he has hugged and kissed Maacha and Tamar, who gives little shouts of joy, which touches me much more than her weeping, after he has hugged and kissed both of them for a long time, he takes me into his arms too. "My little mother," he shouts. "You have become younger." As I put him off laughingly, he says: "I have often thought of you, but the image of you that came to me was always older than you are now, in reality. I am happy to be home again, even though things went well for me in Geshur."

When he comes home on the second or third day, and that means, naturally, to Maacha's home, his happiness has vanished. Distressed, he says: "I wanted to go to the king. Yet in front of the palace were two armed guards who crossed their spears and denied me entry. What does this mean, I asked them. One gave an answer: Prince Absalom's presence is not desired by our lord and king. Not desired today? Not today, not tomorrow, not the day after tomorrow. Do you understand what that means?"

"That your father does not want to see you," explains Maacha tersely, "he has permitted you to come back, but he does not wish to see you."

"Then I probably would have done better to remain with my grandfather in Geshur," says Absalom sadly and lets himself fall onto a couch. He is disturbed, even cries.

"This is Bathsheba's fault," he says. "She wants to push me aside in order to get her son Solomon onto the throne."

He is right, but against Bathsheba and Solomon he is too weak, they are all too weak, even though David loves Solomon least of all his children.

Absalom gets up heavily: "In Geshur I would have been able to become king. It would have been an easy thing for me to inherit my grandfather's throne. There a king—and here, one who is rejected. In Geshur I would certainly not have to beg for the favor of an aging king who dotes on some woman and is no longer entirely in his right mind."

For nearly two years David refused to see his son. Absalom suffered the entire time because of it, I am convinced that his decision to rise up against his father took form at that time.

If Amnon had inherited David's lack of restraint, Absalom had his resoluteness and ability to keep to a plan once made. The rebellion was the last way out. Before that, however, Absalom attempted to get through to David with the aid of his patron, Joab, but now Joab no longer consented to speak with him.

Absalom possessed a farm outside the city and Joab was his neighbor there. Several times the rejected one sent servants to Joab to beg him to discuss matters, but always in vain. Then Absalom ordered his men to burn down a barley field of Joab's that bordered on his fields.

That worked, Joab came.

It is said that Absalom had put himself in front of Joab with arms stretched out wide and shouted: "If the king, my father, will not see me, kill me."

In any event, Joab was so impressed that he promised to talk with David and this time David was willing to receive Absalom.

I was there when the curtain to the throne room was thrown back by two servants and Absalom entered. He prostrates himself upon the floor so that his forehead touches the stone. Slowly David comes up to him, slowly Absalom lifts his head and whispers: "Forgive me, Father, forgive me."

On his so strongly expressive face I can read his horror over David's appearance. He appears old and decrepit at this moment of intense emotion. And yet a great brightness fills his face. He bends down, lifts Absalom up and says: "My son, my darling, my son." Then he takes him in his arms and kisses him.

From this hour on Absalom worked toward a goal that I did not know.

It still took a long time until he acted, time dare not play a role in the attainment of a goal. He continued to live with his mother and from time to time rode out to his estate. He seldom went to the palace. I do not know whether father and son ever saw each other again after their moving embrace and calmly spoke their minds. Absalom despised Bathsheba too much to take the first step and David was probably afraid of her screaming if he let his son come to him too often.

Absalom had a chariot built for himself that was drawn by horses. Horses were from time immemorial a privilege of the royal princes in our country. It hurt around my heart when I thought of Jonathan's single horse Eran. Absalom now possessed a whole stable full of splendid animals.

Whenever he drove out, he had fifty of his brightly clothed servants run along with the chariot as his bodyguard.

People in the streets stood gaping, they were not used to so much display and pomp.

And they admired the handsome man with his luxuriant hair, his proud bearing and the rich adornment that was so completely different from anything they had ever seen in this country.

Absalom soon made friends with Ahithophel, that filled me with fear. I did not know what he intended. But it could not be anything good.

LAST night, I, Michal, had a horrible dream. David and Absalom were fighting with swords over a woman. The woman was Abigail, for me the symbol of the Land of Israel. She stood to the side smiling and I could not tell which of the two she would have liked to see victorious, nor who won.

I awakened and knew: they are all three dead. Pain thrust its way into me, despair. The curse of too long a life, in which the loved ones die off.

If I, Michal, want to tell the story of my life to the end, I must now come to Absalom's uprising.

Even that belongs to my life, naturally, though I myself experienced only our flight. Everything that occurred in Yerushalayim in the meantime I know only from the reports of others. And I will go on, telling it in their words, so that the whole story unfolds, right up to the moment when David and I are once again weeping for one and the same person.

Nothing at all had happened yet, the story began for me when, one day, I passed by the back gate of the palace, where the supplicants were being let in. This time they were crowded together in great numbers.

Against one of the gate-pillars Absalom was leaning, richly clothed, adorned with jewelry, amiable and smiling.

He asked each of the supplicants what city he came from and what brought him here. If it was a man from the north, he said without fail: "Your cause is good and your speech presents it advantageously. But the king will grant you no attention. However, if I were to be installed as judge in this country, so that everyone who had a dispute to present came to me, he would receive a verdict."

As soon as one of the supplicants who had been addressed in this way prostrated himself before him, he lifted the man up and kissed him.

I was alarmed. That was open rebellion. And David sat in his palace without suspecting that Absalom was outside stealing the hearts of the people from him.

Several hours later I meet Absalom at Maacha's dwelling. He puts his arms around my neck and laughs his lighthearted laugh:

"Shocked at me? I tell people only the truth. My father is not a good judge, not any longer. He is old, entirely too busy with his own affairs. I would be a better judge. There are many things in this state that are not as they should be, Bathsheba's influence in affairs. Abominable. Destructive."

He goes on talking, tells of a vow he made in Geshur that if

Jahwe would let him return to Yerushalayim once more, he would celebrate his thanks to him with great feasting and sacrifice in Hebron. Two hundred men had already declared themselves ready to follow him.

I wonder, a vow does not fit well with Absalom who has often made fun when David referred to Jahwe. And why has he waited so long to fulfill the vow? He has been living in Yerushalayim again for almost three years.

He told the same story to David as well, without whose permission he may not absent himself from the city for long. David unconcernedly let him travel to Hebron.

Neither I nor the two hundred who accompanied him knew that Absalom, with the greatest secrecy, had sent couriers to the tribes with the message: when the sound of the trumpet was heard, they should know that Absalom had become king in Hebron.

Why Hebron? Why did he have the rebellion originate in that city? Strategically it was certainly correct. Hebron was still the capital of Judah, David's own tribe. If Hebron and the south fell to Absalom, he thought he would have an easy time in the north.

In Hebron he had come into the world and had spent his early childhood there. Perhaps he also hoped that people there held it against David that he had made Yerushalayim the capital.

Jacob, David's trusted adviser, who visits me from time to time, comes running to me. Breathless, he stands before me: "King David sends me, Princess. Prince Absalom has had himself proclaimed king in Hebron. The majority of the people stand behind him. Dissatisfied with the old, hoping for something new. It is said that he is marching on Yerushalayim at the head of a great army. King David thinks there is nothing left but to take flight. He dares not wait until Absalom lays siege to Yerushalayim and destroys the city. The king wishes that you, Princess, accompany him on the flight."

Two men whom I love oppose each other as enemies. To one I no longer belong, to the other I have never belonged.

As Jacob announces David's wish (or is it David's command) to me, I do not hesitate for a moment, and say yes; yes, I will accompany the king during his flight.

And again resound in me the words of Ruth that had been spoken at my wedding:

> Entreat me not to leave thee,
> Nor to turn back from following thee
> For whither thou goest, I will go also.
> Where thou diest I will die.
> And there will I be buried.

No, I cannot be so disloyal as to desert David now.

Hastily I pack the bare necessities together in a cloth to make a bundle that I can carry easily.

Many people are coming out of the palace and setting off in the direction of the Kidron Valley. David is in the lead, he is barefoot and has covered his head with a thin, gray kerchief. Right behind him walks Bathsheba in a beautiful, white, richly adorned garment, totally unsuitable for taking flight. I see no other wife. Ten of his concubines had been left behind in the palace by David.

In the Kidron Valley David calls a halt. The multitude of the army passes by him, in front, the two priests Abiathar and Zadok, who are carrying the ark of the covenant on two poles like a sedan chair. Zadok, a short, stout man with brown, perfectly round eyes, has not been in this high position very long. I like him better than the fanatic Abiathar.

The two set the chest down and Abiathar says a prayer.

Then David beckons him and says: "Carry the ark of God back into the city. If I find favor in his eyes, he will let me return home. Should he speak thus: I have no pleasure in you, then let him do with me whatever seems good in his eyes."

David speaks further, but now to Zadok: "Return to the city in peace. Ahimaaz, your son, and Jonathan, Abiathar's son, your sons will go with you, I will dwell at the edge of the desert until you send word to me.

Then the two priests turn around with the ark and go back to the city together with their sons.

But the others continued to pass by David, all the Cherethites, all the Pelethites, and six hundred Gittites, behind them their leader, Ittai.

To him David says: "Why are you going with me? Turn back, you are not of my people. You came to me only yesterday. Turn back and bid your people turn back."

Ittai, richly dressed and with iron weapons gleaming in the sun, answers: "As truly as He lives, as truly as my lord and king lives, at the place where he will be, whether in death or in life, there will his servant be."

Then David says to Ittai, and I hear by the slight waver in his voice that he is moved by this faithfulness: "Go then, march on."

Ittai turns about and his men follow him on the difficult road up to the Mount of Olives and into the wilderness.

David walks behind them, lamenting, his head covered like the loyal ones who surround him closely. A dreadful chorus, wild songs of lamentation of the men of Israel, who must flee from their city, from Yerushalayim.

Bathsheba minces along in front of me with tiny steps. Why does she not go faster, I think, she is years younger than I am? Once she stops and then I come alongside her and see, in astonishment, that her face is wet with tears.

"Why are you crying?" She answers, lamenting: "My feet hurt so, my legs, my back, my head."

"Do you want to sit down a bit?" I ask. "Here? in the dirt? So that all the men make fun of me? I am not used to walking. I'm not getting enough air in this heat. My skin is suffering too, my beautiful skin. Isn't yours?" "I am by nature darker than you," I say, "the sun cannot do much to my skin."

"It really does not matter how you look, you don't have to please a husband, a king any longer. How do you come to be here at all?"

"David wished me to."

"He did, did he? Really, sometimes he no longer knows what he is saying or doing."

We hate each other mutually and each is an annoyance to the other during this evil day.

We are now close to David and hear a messenger giving him the news that Ahithophel has come from Gilo and joined Absalom.

As he walks on, David puts both hands in front of his face so that the thumbs and index fingers touch and, with his head thrown back, looks up to the sky and says in a firm voice: "Lord, let Ahithophel's counsel be turned to foolishness today."

We reach the summit where the devout usually prostrate themselves and worship Jahwe. With slow steps, an old man in a hooded cloak comes over the ridge there. The hood is torn, the man has thrown sand in his hair. From people who are standing around, I learn who he is: Hushai, one of David's oldest and most trusted advisers.

David beckons to him with a sad smile. As he speaks, I can hear in his tone how much he likes the man.

"If you go with me, you will only be a burden to me, return to the city and say to Absalom: I will be your servant, O King, your father's servant I was for many years, but now: I am your servant. Zadok and Abiathar, the priests, will be your allies there. It shall be thus: all the talk that you hear in the king's house, report it to Zadok and Abiathar."

David is standing at an angle above me, I see only his figure, gigantic against the bright blue of the sky. Once he was the delicate youth who vanquished Goliath, now he himself has grown and seems to me to be almost a giant. He speaks calmly, accustomed to giving orders, convinced of himself and convincing to the others. That he sent Hushai back to the city proved to be a clever move which saved his sovereignty and destroyed Absalom. Did he want to destroy Absalom? No, but there could be only one victor in this battle.

And thus Hushai returns to Yerushalayim. We move on down the side of the Mount of Olives that faces away from the city, as far as the town called Bahurim, which lies on the edge of the desert.

My heart beats with joy when I see the desert, the refuge of all who flee, again. How I love this wild, barren landscape that glows with a thousand colors.

From Bahurim a man comes running and calls over to us: "I am Shimei, one of the family of King Saul. Whom that one, there, has done out of his throne."

He begins to throw stones at David. A small stone hits me on the left hand, which begins to swell immediately, becomes blue, and hurts, David and Bathsheba are not hit. And so I, the daughter of Saul, am the only one who gets hurt, which causes

Bathsheba to break out in loud laughter. Shimei goes on cursing: "Be gone, man of bloody deeds, man of trouble."

Joab's brother Abishai, the middle one of Zeruiah's three sons, whom I consider even more bloodthirsty than Joab, says to David, "Why should this dog be permitted to blaspheme my lord and king? I will go over and take off his head for him."

David holds him back: "My own son seeks my life, as this one from the House of Benjamin. Let him blaspheme. Perhaps the Lord will then look down upon my misery and let some good be done to me."

Never have I seen David so calm. Slowly I am beginning to comprehend something of his influence over others, his superiority and his gift of being victorious. Probably it is his belief in Jahwe that gives him the strength to bear every adversity with such composure.

I love him very much in these difficult hours.

Is it love? Is it admiration? I cannot say, only that it is a strong feeling that threatens to burst my heart.

I would have liked to sit awhile to catch my breath and weep, but there was no time for that.

Down, down to the meadows by the Jordan. We make preparations to spend the night on the near side, the west bank.

A large tent is erected for David and Bathsheba, a small one, not far away, for me.

Later that evening messengers come from the city, Jonathan and Ahimaaz, the sons of the priests Abiathar and Zadok.

They have been recognized and their presence in the city reported to Absalom. So they had to get away quickly. They hid themselves in a well in Bahurim until Absalom's henchmen had passed. A peasant woman put a cloth over the well and spread out cracked grain on the cloth to dry, so that no one would get the idea that men were concealed in the well. The messengers report that Ahithophel has advised Absalom to set up a large tent on the roof of the palace and lodge the ten concubines of King David there. Then Absalom should go in to them and remain there for some time. In sight of all the people.

David has put his hand over his eyes and says softly: "Thus has my son severed the bond between himself and me." Then he says: "Tell us, what else has happened in Yerushalayim?"

And again Jonathan speaks: "Beyond that, Ahithophel said to Absalom: Give me twelve thousand chosen warriors. With them I will pursue David this very day, while he and his people are exhausted from the march through the desert. I will throw him into a panic so that all the men who are with him flee. Thus I will strike down only the king and bring all the soldiers to you uninjured."

"Thus has Ahithophel spoken, the traitor," says David. "And what has Absalom decided?"

"Absalom said that he found the advice very good, however he wanted to question Hushai as well, because Hushai had come, had thrown himself upon the ground and greeted Absalom respectfully, as one should properly honor a king: Long live the king! Long live the king! Absalom was so impressed that he also wanted to hear Hushai's advice after Ahithophel's. And Hushai said to Absalom: "That is not good advice that Ahithophel gave you. You know your father and his warriors, know how brave they are, beyond that embittered as a she-bear that has had to leave her young alone in the field. Your father will not let his army spend the night out there, he is surely in some hiding place already. I counsel you: Gather to you all the men from Dan to Beersheba, so that their numbers are as great as sand by the sea. You yourself must march along into the confrontation. We will find him and fall upon him like dew upon the clods of earth. Absalom, flattered that he should be there himself, took Hushai's advice, and Hushai reported everything to our fathers. They counsel you, Lord, not to spend the night on the plains of the Jordan whatever happens, but cross over the river, otherwise the king and the army with him are threatened by the danger of being swallowed up."

Jonathan falls silent and looks at David challengingly, as if to ask whether he has really understood. David nods decisively and bids the three leaders Joab, Abishai, and Ittai come to him. They are soon there, David discusses matters with them quickly and quietly.

I have never experienced David as a general and am impressed by how well he leads this difficult maneuver. Not much time remains and yet the crossing of the Jordan is carried out under cover of night. When the sun rises, not a single man has remained behind on the west bank. We move on toward Mahanaim, the two priests' sons accompanying us.

Mahanaim. Hard to say what this city means to me. Unwillingly I once came here, even more unwillingly did I leave again. I see myself riding upon the she-ass that Abner has sent me, and Palti, with his tear-drenched face, running along, at first beside, then behind me.

Now everything is different. Palti is dead, hesitatingly I walk past our house which is standing there empty and neglected. I do not know anyone. Everything is foreign to me and closed up tightly. I no longer belong here. Once, as I am strolling slowly through the streets, someone tugs at my sleeve. A man is standing there and it takes some time until I recognize that it is the messenger who brought me the news of Palti's death.

"Does the Princess wish to know where he is buried?" he asks and adds: "I will lead her there."

I wave him away tiredly. No, I do not want to know where Palti is buried. A grave means nothing to me. I was never at that place with him, he never told me how much he loved me there, for me it is a piece of earth of no importance. The words of Ruth about dying and being buried no longer say anything to me. I will not be buried with Palti and not even with David. It does not even matter to me whether I die in the same place, what matters is to live in the same place and that means together. The older I become, the more surely I know that.

During our flight it has struck me how often now David speaks about being an old man who no longer has much time or much ambition.

I had always thought that growing older was more difficult for a woman who loses her attractiveness for men, now I see that even men have a hard time with getting old, especially active men. Would it have been that way for Palti, that good, modest man? Probably not, but he died at the right time, like Jonathan, they did not have to prove to themselves and others what capable men they were even in old age.

Sadly I walk through the alleys, in which everything appears changed to me. It must be this way to return to a city that war has devastated. Yet there has been no war here, basically everything has remained as it was. So then it is probably I who have changed. As I go farther, I reach the great square in front of Ishbosheth's palace. Here David has called together the leaders and a large part of the army.

He divides the army into three parts. Joab, Abishai, and Ittai, each is to take command of one part. Then David says:

"I, too, will take the field, as supreme commander, to whom all are subordinate."

Then one of the old warriors steps forward and says: "My lord and king, you may not march out with us, for if we should have to flee, they will not have their hearts set on us, and even if half of us were to be killed, they would not care about us. For you, my lord and king, are as ten of our thousands. So it is best if you remain in the city to help if we need it."

Very quietly, quite humbly, David says: "Whatever is best in your eyes I will do." Then he steps back and takes up his position between the pillars at the entrance to the palace.

I listen with astonishment, convinced that he has not always spoken and acted thus.

Now the hundreds and thousands begin to march out and then David says loudly to the leaders, so loudly that everyone can hear it over a wide area: "Deal gently for my sake with the young man, with Absalom."

I lean against the palace wall and weep, weep for David, for Absalom, father and son who love each other, yet each wants to be more than the other and there is no room for that. Everything could still go well, but I do not believe it will. Bad premonitions? Knowledge? A peaceful resolution is not permitted by man, a murderer since the day when Cain struck down Abel because his sacrifice pleased Jahwe more, or supposedly pleased him more, because who can claim to know what Jahwe is thinking?

On whose side is He now? Is He with David? Is He with Absalom?

Lookouts reported that Absalom's troops were crossing the Jordan at the time when we had reached Mahanaim.

Thus there was no question that the battle would be fought in the forests of the east bank, between Mahanaim and the great ford.

The two priests' sons, who had been with us up until now, marched out with the troops commanded by Joab.

We learned later: Ahithophel had mounted his mule immediately on hearing that his advice had been rejected by Absalom and had ridden back to Gilo.

He had scarcely arrived home when he hanged himself. He had probably been the only one who understood that Hushai was acting for David and feared, perhaps not without cause, David's revenge. It occurred seldom among our people that someone killed himself. Our speech has no word for it, one must describe it.

We wait. David, filled with great unrest, walks back and forth between the fortified walls of the city. Infected by his unrest, plagued by evil forebodings, I keep close to him as much as possible.

On one of the towers from which one can see far out into the countryside he has posted a lookout who is to report to him as soon as anyone approaches the city.

Several days of waiting have passed when the lookout reports that a man is coming on the run! David says: "One man alone cannot be fleeing, he is bringing good tidings."

The lookout calls down: "It is Ahimaaz, son of the priest Zadok." "A good sign," says David, "he cannot be bringing bad news."

Ahimaaz throws himself upon the ground before David and says: "Blessed be He, your God, who has delivered over to you the men who had lifted up their hands against my Lord King." "And Absalom?" asks David. "He is well?" "I noticed only a great tumult, but do not know what it meant."

I do not like Ahimaaz's answer, I have the impression that he is keeping something to himself.

Then the lookout in the tower reports a second runner, a Moor. The Moor also throws himself on the ground and says: "Let it be reported to my lord king, He has done justice for you today to all who rose up against you." "And Absalom," David asks again. "Are things well with him?"

The Moor rises slowly, the colored feathers adorning his head wave back and forth. "As it has to the young man, may evil befall all who rise against you."

Then David climbs up to the tower himself, tears his garment to shreds, weeps loudly, and cries out to the city a grim message for all:

> My son Absalom,
> my son,
> my son Absalom,
> would that I had died in your stead,
> Absalom, my son, my son.

I follow him weeping and think that never again will the death of a son be so lamented by a father. Throughout far distant times this lamentation will touch the hearts of men: "Absalom, my son! My son!" Everything, pain and joy, despair and happiness, is more violent, wilder in David than in any other human.

We go into a small chamber in the tower, where there are several stools and a table. A guard-room for soldiers. We sit down, David buries his head in his hands and sobs. We both sit there and cry. Now and then I get up to look down into the city through a narrow slit. There is no victory celebration, even the people are weeping and mourning for the son of the king.

At one point, David sends the lookout down and has a

warrior sent up, whom he questions about the circumstances of Absalom's death.

Then we learn that Absalom was riding on a mule and got his hair tangled in the branches of a large oak tree. The mule, however, ran away from beneath him. A soldier saw him hanging helplessly and reported it to Joab who merely asked why he had not killed the prince. The man said he had not dared to do that, not against the explicit order of the king. He led Joab to the spot and Joab, the butcher, killed Absalom who was hanging there helplessly.

When the soldier has gone, David cries even more.

"Why?" he says. Why? I am startled, the first accusing question to his God.

"Perhaps you loved him too much, David."

He shakes his head violently.

"But it cannot be, that love leads a person onto the path of wickedness."

Why? Again and again people will ask that, uncomprehending, but with ferocious determination to understand it.

"He was so beautiful," says David. "Did Jahwe destroy him because of his beauty? May that which is perfect not exist in the world?"

Blasphemy. There is nothing of: the Lord has given, the Lord has taken away, praised be the name of the Lord.

He lays his head on the table. When he slowly lifts it again, he says calmly: "We owe thanks to Jahwe that he was with us. That, once, perfection came into an imperfect world."

I stand up, walk around the table and stroke David's hair. "Michal," he says, "Michal, I do not deserve this much love from you."

Bathsheba has not let herself be seen in the tower a single time.

When I finally dare to ask David about her, he answers with a pardoning smile: "She bears grief so poorly and therefore is staying away."

"So it is," I say, "but not always the way a woman can do it."

We go on speaking for a long time about Absalom, two grieving parents who have lost their child.

Later Joab enters. I am afraid that David will lunge at him, but he only looks up briefly and goes on crying.

Then Joab says, says it curtly and nastily: "I have known since earlier today that if only Absalom were alive and all of us were dead it would be right in your eyes. Stop lamenting, come down, speak to your people. Otherwise not a single man will spend the night with you. More evil would befall you than all the evil that has come upon you from your youth till today."

David does not look at Joab, he props his head in his hands, remains silent. Suddenly a shudder goes through his body, he straightens up, gets up slowly, climbs heavily down the stairs.

At the entrance to the tower he sits down upon a large rock. Word goes from mouth to mouth, spreads quickly, that he has let himself be seen again, soon all the men march past and salute, not joyfully, his face forbids that, but thankful that he is once again amongst them.

On the next day we set off on the way home, a sorry band of victors.

AUNT ROSA, I, Grete, think to myself and look at the old, white-powdered lady, who is sitting opposite me in a hotel lobby in Jerusalem. And beside her, Mrs. Rosenbaum, the health official's wife, maybe her name was even Rosenbusch, from Ainmillerstrasse, in whose home I lived in a furnished room during my last year in Munich before the emigration. Impossible, she'd have to be much more than a hundred and Aunt Rosa, I know that she died in the U.S. during the war.

I get up, walk slowly by the two women who are conversing in terrible Americanese and announcing loudly *"how wonderful this, our country"* is.

No, naturally it's not they, but it could be. The whole lobby is occupied by this American–Jewish travel group and all, all of them strike me as somehow familiar, coming from the same social level, the upper middle class, they all saved themselves in time or were perhaps even born in the States.

I have nothing to do with them, don't want to have anything to do with them, just as they don't want anything to do with me, I know from experience how much they disapprove of my living in Germany and that they reject my books or, even more, don't even want to read them. They don't want to hear anything more about the time, which, with unintentional irony, they call "the great." They have repressed the persecution, pushed it aside, that happened sometime in the Middle Ages, today, in our civilized, democratic world, such a thing would no longer happen.

So not Aunt Rosa (curious that there's another lady who powders herself so badly), not Mrs. Rosenbaum or -busch. No old acquaintances. Thanks be to Jahwe.

After a long trip through the desert, we arrive to Eilath late Friday evening.

There is not much time to find good quarters and Friday evening everything is filled up. Finally, we find something in a big, but average hotel. Supper for everyone together at a large, opulent buffet. Here live Jews of a stratum (a class?) that I am not used to. No Aunt Rosa, no wife of the health official. They are very oriental, loud, and rude, which disturbs me more in Jews than in other people (an injustice). An atmosphere of petit bourgeoisie hangs over the large dining room.

I have already come across such Jewish petit bourgeoisie, when I worked for the Jewish Council in Amsterdam during the war, in that old theater where those who had been taken from their homes for deportation (in other words, those who were destined for death, which they didn't know for sure, perhaps only had a foreboding) were collected and where, for the whole night, I typed letters for them, in which they asked friends and relatives to send them the necessities, or presumed necessities, for the long trip to the east.

In Eilath, where I run across them again suddenly, I get a shock, cannot get a single bite down, believing that any moment the SS will come marching in and take us all away.

The shock lasts throughout the whole sleepless night, only the next morning does the beauty of the desert drive it away.

I am in Israel for the first time. Again and again I was asked why I, someone who likes to travel so much and often so far, have never been to Israel. I just didn't get around to it, I answered most of the time.

Actually I was afraid of my emotions: I belong there, I don't belong there.

Only after I began to write about Michal did I have the feeling: now I've got to go there.

Not so much because of the landscape, which is really different than in David's time, and I also knew the southern parts of Turkey and Greece, certainly similar and perhaps even "more biblical" regions.

Where my perception failed me was, above all, in the difference in altitudes. Despite good maps, I could only poorly imagine how high, for example, Gibeah is, or was, located, and what you can see from Ophel, the hill where David, and Michal too, lived in Jerusalem.

Now I'm here, my emotions did not get confused, from the first moment on I had the feeling: this is all too foreign, I don't belong here. And although I'm happy to be in Israel, not for a moment do I have the feeling of coming home that I always had in Italy and, above all, in Rome.

Very curious: the Capitoline Hill, which I considered for a

long time to be the most beautiful spot in the world, has nothing, but absolutely nothing at all, to do with me, on the other hand, here in Yad Vashem, my history is very precisely and impressively documented.

I didn't know that one could not find Gibeah at all or only with great difficulty. An approximate idea where it should be looked for. But there no one knew, not Arabs, not Jews. Naturally we pronounced it incorrectly as well. But finally we did come to a hill, covered with stones, a pasture for many sheep with long brown fleeces. And there an Orthodox Jew, who was drawing water from a well, assured us that Gibeah had been here, but was called Tshiva. Nothing from those days has remained, nothing at all.

I have trouble with the places where Michal lived. Mahanaim, on the east bank in Jordan, can't be visited.

Yet I could never have had Michal meet up with an ibex if I had not seen those animals myself, so tame, so without fear of man that you can observe them close-up.

And how could Michal have loved the desert, which I didn't know before this trip and by which I am entranced, by the broad panoramas, the colors and shapes, by the columns of red rock.

En Gedi, where the roses are already blooming at the beginning of March, En Gedi with its waters, steep rocky walls, and the caves in which the young David hid from Saul.

The Mount of Olives on which I'm standing, the huge Jewish graveyard at my feet, where Jews from all over the world wanted to be buried and still do. Where I am standing, Michal stood with David during their flight from Absalom and they, too, looked over toward Jerusalem, even if toward a different one from the one I see.

It is certainly one of the most beautiful views of a city in the whole world.

The golden cupola of the Dome of the Rock dominating, above beautiful mosaics formed of blue and green tiles. The most holy place of the Moslems. Directly below it the most holy place of the Jews, the Wailing Wall (not visible from here), the single remnant of the wall of the Second Temple, destroyed by the Babylonians. The Orthodox men with their big hats and their prayer shawls around their shoulders are standing right next to the Wall or sitting there on narrow chairs.

When you go up to the Wailing Wall, you have to open your handbag to show that there is no bomb or weapon concealed in it.

Oh, if I could only say: I'm a Jew. Jews don't blow things up. But they do. Perhaps this land, promised to them by God, has always made them fighters.

Masada, high, forbidding, lying poignantly above the Dead Sea, where, in the year 72 of our, of the Christian era, the defenders killed themselves, their women and children, in order not to fall into the hands of the besieging Romans: a beautiful, moving, heroic saga, certainly inspiring to children and dear to them throughout their lives. The Israeli soldiers take their oath with the words: Masada will not fall again.

A story, long after Michal, long before me, one that I have not grown up with.

In contrast, the unendingly moving story that comes alive in Jerusalem and by the glorious Sea of Galilee where the blue kingfishers fly, of Jesus, the gentle rabbi who forgave his enemies, with which I grew up just like my Christian schoolmates.

Despite all the foreignness, deep down in my heart a fondness for the country and its inhabitants, a fondness that encompasses the wish that things may go well with them. A wish, in whose fulfillment I do not quite believe.

AND AGAIN a winter has passed. The older I, Michal, become, the faster time goes by. Without anything happening. Day follows day. In peaceful uniformity. Yesterday is like today, there is no difference. Only in my memory do things happen that move me.

Back in my own house in Yerushalayim. I am sitting in the garden in the morning, breathing in the spring air deeply and happily.

Then my maid comes, it is not yet Sulamith, not for a long time yet, and also no longer Rachel, who was with me in the early days of my marriage with David. When I moved away to Mahanaim, she stayed in Gibeah where she had someone she loved. This one is called Judith, is a slender girl with dark, curly hair, who is devoted to me. She comes, bows deeply, is wearing a dress, made of strips of violet and red silk sewn together, that I gave her for her birthday and which she knows I like to see on her. She has golden sandals on her beautiful, slender feet. She is a delightful sight as she now bows again, with her right hand on her breast, and announces to me: "Princess, the king wishes to speak with you." "Which king?" "King David," she says with a soft tone of censure that indicates that there is no other.

My heart beats in my throat, years have gone by, during which David has no longer sent for me. Presumably out of fear of Bathsheba who still rules his days.

I get up carefully and slowly, as I do everything now, my legs no longer have much strength and I am afraid of falling down and breaking something.

In my room, I put a chain of seashells around my neck, as on our first night, and drop essence of myrrh between my breasts.

Do I hope that he will clasp me to himself? Do I wish that? During my preparations I tremble like a girl who is going to her lover for the first time. Look in the bronze mirror and am frightened by the old woman who looks at me with tired, sad eyes, who has so many wrinkles and a sunken mouth.

Why does Jahwe not just let people die? Why does he make them change so before death? And yet feel the same way and think the same way as they did in their youth?

I go over to the palace where a servant receives me and escorts me to David's rooms, which are closed off from the corridor in which we are standing by a heavy curtain. The servant lifts it up for me, I slip through.

There is a splendid view from here out over the broad landscape of spring green, David, too, must be able to look over it from his couch. He is lying propped up on many pelts piled on top of each other, a hollow-cheeked, toothless old man, about whom nothing, nothing at all, recalls Jahwe's angel.

His white hair, which has a trace of yellow, falls over his face in a tangle. Why does Bathsheba not look after him better? His mouth has become hard, the court gossip that he has not laughed since Absalom's death has reached even me. Have I laughed since then? I think not. A sad, embittered David, an unaccustomed sight, deeply disturbing for all.

He snatches at my hand and holds it tightly in his scrawny, old man's hand, blue-veined and covered with brown spots.

"Michal," he says almost in a whisper, hoarse and strained, "my old Michal, what has become of us?" Tears leap into my eyes when he calls me his old Michal. "Much has become of you, David, a great king." "Have I been a great king? Tell me, you are the only one who does not flatter me."

"The greatest king imaginable."

"What is greatness, Michal? Fame for the present? For those who come after us?" Then he goes on speaking rapidly, still just as softly, just as strained: "I have made Yerushalayim the capital and that was good. A city, situated in the center, belonging to no tribe, unites all of them. Its steep hills are unlikely to be captured and not at all in a pitched battle. For that reason I have taken it from the Jebusites.

"I still had many plans, Michal. Therefore I have had the people counted, something with which Jahwe was not in agreement. The prophets spoke only of the seed of Abraham, to whom He has promised this land, they never mentioned numbers. Numbers restrict, are something for merchants, storekeepers, not for a king and quite surely not for Jahwe.

"But I had to know, before I planned my last, great war, how many men capable of bearing arms I had at my disposal. I wanted to send them against all of our enemies, so that, for all time, we could live at peace in this land which is ours.

"If our enemies were to hear how many men I could count on to bear arms, the magnitude of the number would prevent them from attacking us."

"No, David, no. A huge number does not keep the enemy from attacking. I believe that there is only one thing that frightens them and that is the word: war. Each human being must be able to imagine the misery that a war brings to people and if he imagines that, he will not start a war."

"Do you really think so, Michal?"

"Yes, David."

"The people are no longer going along with my plans, they have had enough of killing and being killed. A commander is helpless, is nothing without his warriors. If they will not do anything further, he is paralyzed." He laughs dryly, it sounds like a dog's bark. "They want peace, always just peace, as if that were a possible condition for man."

I bend over him even farther, now he must be able to smell the myrrh. "Why should peace not be possible?" I ask, and within me unfolds the hope that one day there will really be peace. He turns his head away, however: "I have let them become indolent and lazy, that is what takes the luster from my greatness." He trembles, then I hear a strange, lovely sound and see that his harp is hanging above his bed. Our words have caused the strings to resonate. And again I have tears in my eyes. What I would give to hear him play and sing again. But I know that this wish will never be fulfilled.

He says: "I do not believe that Jahwe wants peace for men. The better they live, the more they turn away from him. Even God needs men who believe in him, who serve him."

I say hesitatingly: "If Jahwe is the God I imagine, he does not want war, murdering. Each one should be satisfied with what he has."

"Are you satisfied with your life, Michal?"

That is a frightful question.

"I would have wished another life for myself, David. A life together with you. One in which you would not have had to pay a bride price for me."

"Have you still not forgotten that?"

"I cannot forget that."

"Are things bad for you here?"

"Not that. But not as I would have wished it to be." "Poor little Michal. It is not a good fate, to be a woman." "Have you, David, been able to do everything that you have wished?"

He sits up halfway and says: "Perhaps I really should have built a temple to Jahwe. Now it is too late."

"Jahwe will get his temple. Solomon will build it."

"Solomon?" he says contemptuously, "oh yes, my succesor." He does not say my unloved son, but he thinks it, I can see that. "Do you know, Michal, I have had to make him my successor, I promised his mother." He smiles slyly, draws me down to him and whispers: "She is a slut, but do not tell anyone. She has always been able to wind me around her finger, so great was my desire for her. But even that has passed."

What a sigh he falls back on the pelts.

We do not have much to say to each other, two tremulous old people, disappointed by life. Why is he, too, disappointed? He has accomplished so much. I cannot read him. He is a sealed scroll. Once a shepherd, King of Judah, King of Israel, founder of cities, victorious general, good administrator. The people have it better than ever.

I cannot bring myself to say the two names that were so dear to us both: Jonathan, Absalom. Suddenly I think, full of pain, that Jonathan, too, would be so old, so feeble, so gray.

It is better to die young. But not to be butchered and nailed to a city gate. To die, because nature decrees an end. And that even if, to us, it often appears to be too early. But not to perish by the hand of another man who is greedy for the victim's land, for his goods, his throne. And what will happen to the small nation of the Jews, the prophets of the only, invisible, omnipresent, omnipotent God? To the zealots, those who knew better, in the midst of heathens who worshipped Baal and other gods?

All of a sudden, David sits up: "Michal, give me the harp." I fetch it from the wall, he holds it in his arm, tenderly, as if it were a little child. And he begins to play, a sweet melody that carries me to unimagined heights as once long ago. As beautifully as no other can.

He trembles, opens his mouth like a fish that is vainly gasping for air. Then he says quietly: "I can no longer sing. That is gone. The most beautiful song is within me, remains unsung, even the words no longer form a song, gone, gone." Tears run from his eyes. I kneel down before him and lay my head in his lap. He strokes my hair. But suddenly he puts the harp aside, sobbing wildly, falls back, and now he embraces me completely.

Quietly we lie together, stroking, kissing each other. Knowing what we have missed. Once he asks: "Why have you not had a child by the other man?"

"David, for Palti I was always your wife."

"You did not sleep together?" Disbelieving, horrified.

"You stood between us."

He asks: "Did you not like him?" "I was very fond of him, David. He was the best human being I have known." "Poor

Michal, dear Michal." And sobbing, he sucks firmly at my mouth. And so we lie there a long while, aroused and happy, try to make up for what we have missed.

After a very long time, he pushes me away gently and hands me the harp. I take it and hang it on the wall again.

I stand in front of the couch with arms crossed, then I hear a noise. Bathsheba is standing in front of the curtain, clad in white, draped with jewelry, a wave of coldness breaks against me. I think, frightened, what would she have done if she had come in earlier?

Her cutting voice. "What are you doing here?" "I had her summoned," says David humbly, as if he had to account to her.

"So, you had her summoned. Behind my back. What is going on here?" "She is my wife." "Your wife? I am that, too." "But she is the first, the first wife with whom I slept, you must understand that."

"You have become childish," she says harshly, "what does it matter if one is the first one?" "She was. I loved her." "That is a long time ago. And she did not bear you a child. A woman without children is worth nothing."

He says nothing, nor do I. Go slowly to the curtain. There I turn around to David once more. Look at him a long time and know that it is for the last time.

I turn away, lift the curtain, leave the room, behind me the heavy fabric slides back into place.

My feeling was correct, I did not see David again. He became sick, suffered from chills that could not be alleviated by any means. Then he died.

Solomon ascended the throne, built this ostentatious palace for himself. I did not want to live in it, but I was not asked.

Bathsheba had my house taken away. Other people moved in. That was years ago.

As long as I live here, I live in fear of her and tell my story to myself as a consolation. And love the dead David as I did the living one. Mourn for the music that died with him, that means more to me than his greatness, which belongs to the world.

⠶ *I*T IS getting to be time for me, Grete, to depart from this story. Michal has left David, the curtain has fallen on her life, her love.

The question of what David really was, with which I began this story, remains unanswered. His figure disappears in the darkness of history.

Probably he resembled neither the David of Michelangelo nor that of Rembrandt.

I still find Michelangelo's David beautiful, but I would no longer hang his picture in my room in order to carry on a dialogue with him.

Rembrandt's Jewish boy is closer to me, I would like to press him, who seems destined to suffer, who would not have survived Auschwitz, to my sorrow-filled heart.

The real David, my ancestor, foreign to me, close to me.

He and Michal did not know what fate awaited their, our

people. I envy them that. I, the late-born, must bear the knowledge of Auschwitz to the end of my life, it will torment me till
my last breath.

Like Michal's life, my life is also over. Not much more will
happen beyond the one thing about which I, who have liked
reporting about everything, will no longer be able to report:
my own death.

About the Author

Grete Weil was born in 1906. She married Edgar Weil in 1932, and emigrated with him to Holland. He was arrested in 1941 and died in a concentration camp. Grete Weil went into hiding in 1943, survived, and returned to Germany in 1947. She has published four novels and two short story collections, and now lives near Munich.

Bride Price

was set in Fournier, a font named after the eighteenth-century typographic pioneer who was instrumental in applying rationalistic (and occasionally even mathematical) principles to type design. The consistency of his approach is seen in the smoothness and elegance of his Roman letters, with their perpendicular shading and narrower set width, and his italic is notable for its regular and consistent slope. Fournier, along with Bodoni and Baskerville, formed a bridge between the old style letters of the sixteenth and seventeenth centuries and the new style, more modern forms that would be introduced in the nineteenth. But unlike Bodoni and Baskerville, Fournier was concerned with designing a type that would work well for trade books and not deluxe limited editions. In Fournier he achieved a type that looked narrow, but not emaciated, elegant, but not affected.

The book was set by Huron Valley Graphics, Ann Arbor, Michigan, and has been printed and bound by Haddon Craftsmen, Scranton, Pennsylvania. It was designed by Caroline Hagen.

DATE DUE

DEMCO 38-297